MONTANA SEAL

BROTHERHOOD PROTECTORS

NEW YORK TIMES BESTSELLING AUTHOR
ELLE JAMES

Ebook ISBN: 978-1-62695-151-8

Print ISBN: 978-1-62695-152-5

Dedicated to my readers who make my dreams come true by keeping me in the business I love dearly...WRITING! I love you all so much. Thank you for buying my books!

Elle James

AUTHOR'S NOTE

Visit ellejames.com for titles and release dates
and join Elle James's Newsletter

CHAPTER 1

"Don't get too far ahead, Con Man." Chief Petty Officer Trevor Anderson studied the terrain, searching for any signs of trouble.

"Why the hell are we out here, anyway?" Mason "Con Man" Connolly asked. "I thought we'd pretty much cleaned out the Taliban influence from this corner of Afghanistan. Hell, we didn't see anything this afternoon when we performed our weekly walk-through."

"You know the guys in Intel. They think everyone is out to screw the US government. They're on a witch hunt for dirty contractors."

"Is that why we're out here in the dark? They think we're going to catch some contractor making dirty deals?" Jay C said into Trevor's headset. "Why didn't they say so in the briefing?"

"They didn't want word to get out before we left

the tactical operations center," Trevor said. "The fewer people who know why we're out here, the better chance we have of catching those involved."

"You think there are traitors among our folks?" Connolly asked.

Trevor's jaw tightened. "It happens more often than you might think."

Connolly snorted. "Bastards."

"I'll kill them with my bare hands." Tank said.

"I could be back in my cot, catching some Zs instead of tromping around in the sand," Rutherford muttered. "And you know how I hate to miss my beauty sleep."

"It's bad enough we have to deal with the Taliban," Cage said. "We shouldn't have to deal with our own crooked citizens."

"You're preaching to the choir, man." Trevor glanced at his watch. "We're meeting with some of the local leaders to discuss the issue under the cover of night to maintain their anonymity. But that doesn't mean we won't encounter hostiles. Keep your eyes peeled. I'm coming up behind you, Con. Jay C hang back. Tank, Rutherford, Cage, follow me."

"I'll be glad when we get back to conducting real assignments, preferably involving water." Cage slipped up beside Trevor. "The sand in all my cracks is really beginning to chafe." For a long moment, he stood still, scratching his arms, legs and groin through the fabric of his uniform.

Trevor ignored the sand in all his crevices and focused on the task at hand. He'd had orders to hold off telling his men about the real mission until they were well underway. The CO suspected a leak in the command center, feeding data to the traitor. He wanted the team to get a head start on the mission before anyone else knew what was going on.

Intel had set up a meeting between his team and some of the local leaders who were supposed to receive reconstruction payments from some of the US government representatives working in the area. The question was, what were they receiving compared to what the contractors were reporting? If there were discrepancies, someone had to be held accountable.

Unfortunately, when an independent surveyor had gone out to question the people receiving the money, he hadn't returned. They located his body, picked clean by buzzards, his bones left to bleach in the hot desert sun.

"We're here to ask questions, not to expend ammo. Keep that in mind. The local leadership will be distrustful as it is, with us carrying full battle rattle, armed to our teeth."

"So, we're here to show our support and get the real poop on what's happening," Connolly said. "Check." He paused. "I see some people coming out of the village. Moving closer."

Trevor tensed. "Don't give yourself away. We're

3

closing the distance." He nodded toward his teammates and jerked his head toward the direction they'd be moving. "Let's go. And maintain radio silence until we're close enough to—"

"See the whites of their eyes?" Connolly chuckled. "What era did you grow up in? John Wayne's been gone a long time."

Trevor grinned. During the long cold months of winter in Montana, his father had watched just about every old western ever made. Trevor could just about recite every line of every John Wayne movie script. "Shut up and keep an eye out for trouble."

"On it, boss," Connolly said. "And don't be so grumpy."

"Who said I was grumpy?" Trevor said with a little more bite than intended.

"Ever since Con Man got the girl, you've been a grump," Tank responded. "Admit it."

"She should have chosen me," Trevor muttered. His heart still squeezed hard in his chest over his loss, even after nearly a year. Lana had been friends with both of them. They had been The Three Musketeers. Then one night, Trevor had kissed Lana, and everything changed. He'd wanted her so badly, he could barely eat or sleep for thinking about her. She'd started dating both men, admitting she'd had a hard time choosing between them.

When it came down to it, Con Man had asked her to marry him before Trevor. Trevor had wanted his

4

proposal to be perfect. He'd purchased the ring and made reservations for a fancy restaurant and planned everything.

Except Connolly beat him to her. He'd picked her up from her work one day and driven down to the beach. From what Connolly had described, they'd walked hand in hand, and he'd gotten down on one knee, proposing to her as the sun melted into the ocean.

Yeah, one freakin' year, and Trevor still wanted to be with Lana.

"Well, she chose me," Connolly said. "But if anything should happen to me, you'll be there to take care of her, right?"

"Damn straight," Trevor said. "Perhaps we should focus on our mission here and move in closer. Eventually, we'll have to come out and greet our liaisons."

"Moving," Connolly said.

The men leap-frogged from bush to bush, clinging to the shadows to make certain no one with a sniper rifle could pick them off.

The briefing in the tactical operations center had indicated the team would be heading west to check on a possible group of Taliban insurgents setting up camp near the hills.

As soon as the helicopter from the 160th Night Stalkers took off, it veered in the opposite direction, heading east.

The pilot had the GPS coordinates where they

were to meet with tribal leaders from an Afghan village to interview them in secret. The Navy SEALs were to conduct the mission, making certain the local leaders were safe, and then get back with the information.

"See anything?" Trevor asked.

"Only what looks like three Afghan leaders walking out of the village toward me with two armed guards, one on either side of the group," Connolly said. "Twenty yards away from me and closing."

"Stay hidden until I catch up to you. I'll be the one to step out and greet them." Trevor nodded toward Tank.

Tank grunted. "I've got your back."

With his buddy's reassurance, Trevor zigzagged through the darkness from shadow to shadow. He'd only gone ten yards when a loud explosion ripped through the air, and all hell broke loose.

The village leaders hit the ground, their guards dropping along with them.

"Get down!" Trevor shouted, though he didn't have to. His men knew when to hit the dirt and when to come out fighting.

For two, maybe three minutes, bullets flew.

"Where are they coming from?" Trevor spoke into his mic.

"All around," Tank said. "No tracer rounds to locate origin."

"Can any of you move back?"

"Working on it," Jay C said. "I'm furthest back. I'll swing wide and find out where the bullets originate."

"Sounds like several rifles and a machine gun," Rutherford bit out.

"And what the hell bomb was that?" Cage asked. "Everyone still with us?"

"This is Anderson. Sound off with status," Trevor commanded.

While the bullets continued to fly over their heads, the men of his team chimed in.

"Cage, here."

"Jay C, alive and kickin'."

"Tank, with you."

"Rutherford, free of lead so far."

A moment of silence reigned between the barrage of bullets.

"Connolly?" Trevor prompted. "Report."

Nothing. Then the machine gun gave that deadly burping sound as it expelled multiple rounds in rapid succession. Rifle fire recommenced, and the insurgent fire continued.

Up until that point, Trevor had been steady, calm and collected, focused on surviving and continuing his mission. But when his wingman and best buddy, Connolly, hadn't checked in, his heartbeat ratcheted up, and his chest grew so tight he could barely draw a breath. "I'm going after Con Man."

"Hold on," Tank said. "Let me catch up to you and provide cover."

Trevor couldn't wait. If Connolly was injured, he might be bleeding out. The sooner he got to him, the better chance he had of keeping his friend alive.

"Can't wait." Trevor pushed to his feet and ran in a crouching position. When bullets kicked up dust near his boots, he dove to his belly and continued toward Connolly in a low crawl, keeping his head as low as possible.

"Damn, Anderson," Tank said into his earbud. "You make it hard for a guy to cover your back."

"Got to…" he said, using his knees and elbows to propel his prone body across the rugged ground, "get to…Connolly." The going was arduous, but nothing would stop Trevor. He thought he was getting closer to the last point he'd seen his friend, but it was hard to tell with only the stars shedding light on the ground and his vision limited to no more than a foot above the ground. He adjusted his night vision goggles and spied a glowing green image.

At the next bush, he ran into a lump lying in the shadows.

"Connolly," he choked out, his words lodging on the constriction in his throat.

His friend lay still.

Trevor scooted across the dirt to lie in the dark beside his fellow SEAL, his hands and arms slipping through warm, sticky blood. "Connolly, stop fooling around and talk to me, man." His eyes burned as he felt for a pulse at the base of Connolly's neck. For a long moment, he felt nothing. Then a hand reached up and grabbed his arm.

"Anderson," Connolly whispered, the name coming out as a gurgling sound.

Trevor leaned close to his friend's mouth to listen over the sound of the gunfire all around. He didn't dare turn on a flashlight. Any light at that point would only provide more of a target for the shooters. Instead, he ran his hand across Connolly's chest and unbuckled the bulletproof vest. Inside, his uniform was dry. "Where are you hurt?"

"You have to...get...out...of here," Connolly said, the sound barely loud enough to be heard over the melee.

"I'm not leaving without you," Trevor said.

"You have to." Connolly's hand tightened on Trevor's arm. "Go."

"Not without you," Trevor insisted. "Lana would never forgive me."

"Lana," Connolly's hand slid off Trevor's arm and fell to his side. "She loved us both."

"Yeah, so don't disappoint her. She expects you to come back in one piece."

"We talked...about having kids...someday." Connolly lay still for a long moment.

No matter how hard Trevor searched, he couldn't find the wound on Connolly's front side. He pulled his friend's arm in an attempt to roll him onto his side.

His friend resisted, albeit with little strength. "No. It's too late."

"No, it's not." Trevor cupped the back of Connolly's head. "You're coming home. Alive."

His friend shook his head. "Home, yes. Alive? Not so much. Take care of her." He touched Trevor's arm, and then his hand slid away, falling back to the earth. "Take care of Lana. She'll need help. But she won't ask for it."

"What do you mean, she'll need help?"

"She'll feel guilty."

"Why?"

"She didn't just love me," Connolly said, his voice fading. His eyes widened, the whites glowing in the darkness. He reached up, his hand gripping Trevor's arm in a sudden display of strength and determination. "Promise you'll take care of her."

"You're coming home to take care of her yourself," Trevor insisted. "You're coming home."

"Promise, damn it." Connolly half-lifted his head from the ground, his grip on Trevor's arm tightening.

"Okay, I promise," Trevor said. "But you're not leaving me, man. I won't let you."

"You don't get that choice."

Trevor had to lean close to catch Connolly's last words.

The hand on his arm slipped free and fell to the ground. Connolly lay still.

His pulse pounding, Trevor touched his fingers to

his friend's neck, praying for a pulse. All noise and commotion around him seemed to fade into the background.

Nothing.

No pulse.

He leaned close to his friend's mouth and nose hoping to feel the gentle puff of breath against his cheek.

Again, nothing.

"Anderson, the attackers are moving out." Rutherford reported. "How's Connolly?"

Oh, he'd found Connolly, but too late to help him. "I found him."

"I have a call into the Night Stalkers. They're on their way now to cover and extract," Cage, their radio operator said. "Should be here in two mikes."

Taking a deep breath, Trevor ordered, "Move to the extraction point."

"We'll move when you move," Cage said.

"Damn straight," Rutherford agreed.

"What about Connolly?" Tank asked quietly.

"I'll bring him out. Cover me in case the enemy hasn't left the area all together."

"Will do," Tank said.

"I've got your back," Cage said.

"Me, too," Jay C piped in.

"All of us," Rutherford ended. "Looks like the attackers bugged out."

"I'm on my way." Trevor said. He took hold of

Connolly's arm and pulled him up and over his shoulder in a fireman's carry, his friend's body a dead-weight.

Dead.

Trevor's heart hurt so badly, he could barely take a step. But he had a promise to keep. Connolly wanted him to look out for his wife. Lana would be devastated over her loss. Not that Trevor would take advantage of it, but he couldn't let her weather the loss alone. They'd been friends and still were. And friends stood by each other during bad times.

With his teammates covering him, Trevor carried Connolly's body to the extraction point.

Tank and Jay C, under the cover of Rutherford, checked on the village leaders.

They reported back that all three leaders and their guards were dead. Not only had they failed in their mission to gather data, they'd failed to keep their informants alive.

As Trevor laid Connolly's body on the floor of the Black Hawk helicopter, his jaw tightened, anger burning a black hole in his heart.

The only way they could have been surprised so thoroughly was if someone had prior knowledge of their meeting. Someone who'd set up an elaborate trap intent on killing anyone who could expose the shady dealings the contractors were pulling on the locals.

Someone on the inside had access to their coordinates and secret operations plans.

Inside the wire surrounding the camp, they had a traitor, and that traitor was responsible for Connolly's death.

CHAPTER 2

A YEAR LATER...

LIFE POST-MILITARY COULDN'T BE MORE different.

Trevor lost his love for the fight after Connolly's death and the funeral that had ripped out his heart. He'd begged Lana to let him stay with her until she got stronger, but she'd sent him back to his unit, saying they needed him more.

His brothers-in-arms were just as much family to Connolly as she had been, she said. Maybe more so. They needed him to help them through their loss.

Trevor had gone back to his position, but when the time came for him to re-up and sign on for more of the same had come due, he couldn't put his name on the dotted line. Instead, he'd submitted his paperwork to exit the military.

Fortunately, he had a friend in Montana who'd heard of a start-up organization that provided protective services to paying clients and other worthy individuals. It was in his home state of Montana, and he could use some of the skills he'd learned in Navy SEAL BUD/S training. He'd signed up without hesitation.

Thus, began his employment with the Brotherhood Protectors, working for Hank Patterson, a former Navy SEAL.

He couldn't have landed a more perfect job. After all, what else was he good for? All he knew was tactics, battle skills and weaponry. His cowboy skills were rusty from being dormant for so many years. But that, was just what Hank Patterson was looking for—the battle skills, coupled with a strong sense of honor and a solid work ethic.

Born and raised in Montana, Trevor had those two traits in spades. Except he feared he might be lacking in the honor area. His friend had died, and all he could think about was wanting to be with his friend's widow. Guilt ate at him like a flesh-eating disease. When Lana had told him he didn't have to stick around, he'd taken her at her word, choosing to leave her alone rather than risk showing his love for her. She deserved her time to grieve without being pestered by someone who was perpetually lovesick for her.

He'd been vigilant in checking up on her, calling

her once a month and on her birthday to hear her voice and get a feel for how she was doing since her husband's death.

Trevor had quit the Navy and returned home to Montana.

Life seemed to be settling onto an even keel, though the survivor's guilt never seemed to dissipate. Trevor hoped, with time, the pain of loss would fade.

After his first assignment with the Brotherhood Protectors in Eagle Rock, Montana, Trevor went fly fishing with one of his new friends on the team, Chuck Johnson. While he'd been out, he'd received a call from Lana. He hadn't been in range of a cell phone tower when the call had come through, but she'd left a message.

He and Chuck made it back to the Blue Moose Tavern in Eagle Rock before his cellphone pinged, indicating voice mail.

"Trevor, it's Lana." She paused briefly. "I might be in a little bit of trouble. I could use your help. But if you can't make it, I'll understand." She paused again. "On second thought, don't worry about me. I've got this. Forget I called." The message ended abruptly. He stared down at his phone, frowning.

"What's wrong?" Chuck lifted his beer but didn't take a swig. "Girl troubles?"

"Not mine," he answered automatically. "My former teammate's widow."

"She's in trouble?"

Trevor nodded. "Sounds like it, but she ended by saying forget about it."

"Huh. That's when the trouble's deeper than she can imagine, and she's so deep she doesn't want to pull you into the mess." Chuck set his mug on the bar. "Call her back."

Trevor tapped Lana's number and pressed the phone to his ear. After seven rings, he shook his head. "No answer."

"Man, you need to go," Chuck said.

Trevor nodded. "Yes, I do. I made a promise to her husband I'd look out for her."

"And that's what we do. Special Ops guys look out for their own and the ones they love." Chuck slid off his bar stool and stood. "Need my help?"

"I don't know yet. I'll have to get down to San Diego ASAP and reconnoiter the situation." Trevor slapped a bill on the counter and stood. "What's the fastest way to get a plane out of here?"

Chuck grinned. "Talk to Hank. He has friends in all the right places."

Trevor had to call Hank anyway to tell his new boss he'd be skipping town without a projected return date.

Hank had been more than understanding, offering to hook him up with a buddy who owned an airplane. All he had to do was help pay for fuel, and within five hours of receipt of Lana's call, he was well on his way to San Diego.

Hank had even arranged for a rental car to be waiting at his destination airport. Darkness had long since cloaked the land, but the bright streetlights in California reminded Trevor of why he loved Montana. Here, every street corner had a brightly shining light while back home the moon and stars provided the only illumination needed. He drove through the streets, reminding himself to ease his foot off the accelerator. Getting a speeding ticket would only slow him down more.

When he finally pulled to a stop in front of the townhouse Lana and Connolly had called home, his pulse kicked up, and his hands grew damp on the steering wheel. He hadn't spoken face-to-face with Lana since the funeral. Would he still feel the same attraction he'd felt since their first kiss? Would he be able to hide his feelings for the woman? Could he present a sense of friendship with no strings attached in his bid to help her with whatever trouble she'd run into? The last thing he wanted was for her to feel uncomfortable around him.

The only way he'd know the answers to any of those questions was to get out of the vehicle, march up to the door and find out for himself.

He glanced at the section of the building he'd visited so many times when Connolly and Lana had invited him over to dinner. A quick look at his watch indicated it was almost midnight. Lana would be in bed by now.

Trevor stepped out of the vehicle.

A light glowed from the upstairs bedroom he knew to be the master bedroom where Lana and Connolly had slept.

Did she sleep with the lights on? Was she that insecure since her husband's death?

His chest tightening, Trevor took a step toward the door. He'd put off seeing her in person for far too long. She'd insisted she didn't need him, but she might have been hiding her grief to spare him.

Trevor could have kicked himself for his selfishness. He shouldn't have left Lana alone for so long. He'd made a goddamn promise to Connolly and had failed him.

As he strode toward the door, Trevor noticed a shadowy movement through the window of the first floor where the blinds were open but the room beyond lay in darkness.

A familiar prickly sensation tingled down the back of Trevor's neck, alerting him. Something wasn't right in Lana's house.

He looked up at the window of the master bedroom and froze. A woman stood in front of the window. The drapes were drawn, but the light from inside silhouetted her figure. She tugged at her top, lifting the hem up her torso and pulling it over her head before tossing it aside.

When she turned, her perky breasts were nothing but shadows, but they had the same effect on Trevor as if he'd seen her in the flesh. His groin tightened automatically.

Then the shadowy figure on the first floor drew his attention back to the problem at hand.

Did Lana have a guest in her house? Or was the dark figure an intruder?

Not willing to wait until something awful happened to Lana, Trevor raced for the townhouse and tried the front door. It was locked. If the figure was an intruder, he had to have entered through a door or window at the rear of the structure.

The townhouse was one of several in a row. The only way to go around to the back was to circle four or five other townhouses. Trevor couldn't spare that kind of time. The figure on the first floor had made it to the stairs.

Trevor studied the front of the brick townhouse. A polished bronze, metal trellis covered in colorful bougainvillea stretched up the front of Lana's unit, almost all the way up to her bedroom window.

He didn't hesitate. The person inside would make it to Lana's bedroom before Trevor could think through any other alternative. He had to act.

Trevor placed his foot on the bottom rung of the metal trellis and tested it for stability. Then he was climbing, hand over hand, up the side of the townhouse to the top of the trellis. He couldn't quite make it to the window ledge using the trellis. Reaching to the side, he gripped the brick ledge of the windowsill and pulled himself up then stared through the curtained window into the room inside.

Although his sight was blurred by the curtain, he could see Lana standing beside the bed. Her head jerked toward the window at the same moment the bedroom door exploded inward.

She emitted a scream and grabbed the lamp on the nightstand.

Trevor tried to lift the window, but it didn't budge.

Inside the bedroom, a man dressed in black advanced on Lana, carrying what appeared to be a weapon in his hand.

"What do you want?" she called out.

He didn't answer. Lana dropped to the floor a moment before the sound of gunfire rent the air.

Trevor cocked his elbow and slammed it into the window. The glass shattered inward. Trevor pulled himself as far to one side of the window as possible.

Another shot was fired, this time at the window, shattering even more glass.

Lana popped up from the floor and flung a pillow at the intruder, then ducked back down.

Knowing he had only seconds, Trevor couldn't take the time to clean the jagged shards out of the way. He curled his body into a tight ball and rolled through the window onto the floor.

As soon as he hit the ground, he rolled behind the bed, landing close to where Lana hunkered low, wearing nothing but her bra and panties, her body shaking. She cocked her arm, ready to throw her elbow into him when he caught her around the middle.

"It's me, Trevor," he said.

More shots were fired. One pierced the bed and nicked Lana's arm.

She gasped and lay flatter against the floor.

Outside the townhouse, sirens sounded.

A muttered curse sounded from the other side of the room, and footsteps crossed the floor, heading toward them.

Catching Lana's wide-eyed gaze, Trevor pressed a finger to his lips, bunched his muscles and prepared to launch himself at the intruder.

When the man rounded the end of the bed, Trevor threw himself at the guy's knees, knocking him off his feet.

The two crashed to the floor.

Trevor had seconds before the man regained his senses. He grabbed the wrist holding the gun and slammed it against the floor. The weapon went off twice before the man loosened his grip and the gun slid free.

Lana emerged from behind Trevor and dove for the gun. She came up on her haunches, pointing the weapon at the man.

Downstairs, someone banged on the door to the

townhouse. The next moment a crash sounded below.

"It's the police!" A man shouted. "Put your weapons down and come out with your hands up!"

"On the second floor," Lana called out. "We have the intruder pinned to the floor. Please, come help."

Footsteps pounded on the steps leading to the second floor of Lana's townhouse. Moments later, two uniformed policemen edged around the doorframe, weapons drawn.

"Miss, put the weapon down," said the first officer through the door as he pointed his weapon at Lana.

"She's not the perpetrator," Trevor said, pressing his arm across the real criminal's throat. He dipped his head toward the intruder. "He is."

"We'll take over," the officer said. "As soon as the lady releases the weapon."

Lana laid the handgun on the floor and shoved it toward the officer.

He kicked it back to the second officer and shifted his aim toward Trevor and the man on the floor. "We'll handle this."

The man beneath him bucked, fighting to free himself.

"You want me to let him go?"

"Yeah, let him go. We'll take it from here."

"Lana, get back," Trevor warned. He wasn't sure what the man would do when he released his hold.

Taking a deep breath, Trevor rolled over and onto his feet, remaining in a crouched, ready position.

The intruder leaped to his feet and plowed into the first police officer like a lineman tackling the opposing quarterback, knocking him backward.

The officer went down, taking his partner with him.

The perpetrator raced out of the bedroom and down the steps.

Trevor leaped over the officers and went after the guy. He wouldn't let him get away. Not after he'd tried to kill Lana. The man couldn't be allowed to run loose on the streets. He could make another attempt on Lana's life.

Not on Trevor's watch. He'd promised Connolly he'd take care of Lana. It was about time he lived up to his word.

LANA STOOD IN THE BEDROOM, shaking from head to toe. Never in her life had she been shot at. Now, she had an idea of what Mason and Trevor had been up against every time they'd gone on a mission. Only they'd faced more than one adversary, each wielding a high-powered rifle or machine gun. Not one lone gunman with a pistol.

Trevor.

Oh, sweet Lord. Trevor had come just when she'd needed him most.

Her heart hammered against her ribs, and her cheeks flushed with heat.

Lana had loved Mason with all her heart. And she'd loved Trevor, too. But she'd married Mason, not Trevor.

Their friendship had suffered because of her choice, but she couldn't marry both men, and she'd wanted a regular life with a family filled with children. She and Mason had talked about trying to get pregnant after he'd returned from his last deployment.

That same lead ball settled in the pit of her gut. No matter how much time passed, she still couldn't think about the casualty assistance officer who'd showed up at her door to deliver the news of Mason's death.

Trevor had arrived days later to hold her as she'd cried her heart out. He'd been there through Mason's funeral and the week following, after which, she'd sent him away. She'd told herself she needed time to grieve alone, to get her head on straight, to learn to live without Mason.

That had been a year ago. A year she'd gone without seeing Trevor. A year she'd pushed him away with every phone call. And with one text, poof! He'd come.

Warmth spread through her chest, and she could finally move.

"Backup just arrived," one officer said. "Will you be all right?"

She nodded. "Go. Help Trevor catch the bastard."

The officers scrambled to their feet and ran after Trevor.

Lana dressed quickly in a T-shirt and shorts, left her room and descended the staircase, holding tightly to the railing, her legs feeling like wet noodles, refusing to work the way they were intended. She couldn't fall apart. Not now. Not when she was obviously getting close to the truth.

Why else would someone come after her with a gun? She wasn't stupid, thinking the attack had been a random break-in. The masked gunman had come after her, specifically.

She hurried to her purse and rifled through it, breathing a sigh of relief when she felt the smooth metal surface of her light-weight laptop.

Thank goodness, he hadn't gone after it. She kept all the data she'd collected on that laptop. Fortunately, she also kept a backup on the internet cloud. If something happened to her—and if anyone cared—they could find what she'd discovered by going through her files.

Assuming anyone dug deep enough to learn why she'd been targeted in the first place. She hadn't yet gone to the police or the FBI with the information she'd been collecting. In her mind, she'd been waiting for clear proof, beyond a shadow of a doubt, before she turned it over to any government agency. Only then would they believe her. But she was getting so close, she figured she was in way over her head.

So, she'd set up the meeting with the FBI. She hadn't asked her coworker to join her in her big reveal. A couple months ago, Peter Bishop had happened upon her digging into a database she shouldn't have been in. She'd felt obligated to tell him what she was looking for.

Peter had been shocked by her revelation that something illegal was going on inside their organization, and that someone might be plotting against the government. He'd promised not to tell anyone and had offered to help her in her investigation.

His computer skills were much better than hers, and he'd managed to hack into some of the more restricted government databases, revealing even more connections between the contractors working the reconstruction projects in Afghanistan and people stateside who had dealings with anti-government groups. Some of those anti-government organizations were loosely linked to several bombing incidents in the Pacific Northwest and in Boston.

Those groups with their coded conversations made Lana nervous when she lurked on their social media sites.

That's when she'd decided the information she'd dug up was dangerous. But to reveal the data was a huge step.

She stood a good chance of losing her job over the information she'd ferreted out of the Department of Homeland Security and other government databases she had no business poking into. But what she'd learned was way too alarming to keep to herself. She had to let someone know.

Her biggest fear was that they'd chalk up her findings as belonging to a crazed conspiracy theorist. Who would believe her if she told them her husband's death in Afghanistan had been to confuse and cover up a terrorist's plot? A plot that involved a potential attack on American soil—an attack aimed at the ultimate overthrow of the US government? And that the effort was linked to a high-ranking official in an agency set up to protect the country from such attacks?

Even she'd had a hard time believing it. Mason's last words to her—besides *I love you*—had been *We're going out to nail some crooked Americans.* He'd sworn her to secrecy because he wasn't supposed to tell her about his missions. She wasn't to tell anyone, including Trevor, their best friend, what she knew. Mason had eavesdropped on a secret conversation by accident. He'd known why they were going on his last mission, despite what his commander had told them. "And I have a good idea who they are."

After almost a year, and after going to work for the Department of Homeland Security, Lana had names of those she suspected were responsible for her husband's death and for the ongoing planning of a potentially deadly terrorist attack scheduled to take place in the US.

Lana had taken the next step. That morning she'd contacted the district office of the FBI and set up a meeting for the following day. When asked the nature of the meeting, she'd hedged. As an executive secretary to Huntley Powell, a high-level, regional director of the DHS, she didn't want to out-and-out accuse anyone over the phone. She wasn't certain whether they would spill her story to the world or sweep it under the rug. Either way, she was putting herself out there and was in danger because of what she knew, and she could be exposing herself to the organization where she worked.

Now, she was certain someone had caught wind of her findings. She wouldn't be safe in her own home. Not until she exposed the people involved.

Even before the two policemen made it out the door, more arrived through the front.

"Ma'am, are you all right?"

She nodded. "I'm okay."

"We got word shots were fired. An ambulance is on the way," the lead officer said.

"I don't need an ambulance, but you might check the neighbors. The gunman fired several rounds. I don't know where all of them went."

The policeman talked with three other officers

who'd arrive. Those three split up and headed for the neighbors on either side of Lana's townhouse.

An ambulance arrived moments later, and an EMT jumped to the ground and hurried toward her, carrying what appeared to be a medical kit.

The police officer intercepted him and told him she wasn't harmed, but to check on her anyway.

The EMT gave Lana a brief smile. "Do you mind if we check you over. Sometimes, the shock of an assault makes people unaware of their injuries. They don't always realize they're hurt."

"I'm not bleeding..." Lana ran her hands up her arms and stopped when her fingers touched something wet and sticky. She held her hand in front of her and felt her knees weaken again.

"Ma'am, could you please take a seat until my guys can unload the stretcher?" He led her to the sofa and gently pressed on her shoulder.

Lana sat before her knees gave out. "Really, I'm okay," she said, though her voice shook, not sounding very convincing. "I don't need a stretcher. I'm more worried about Trevor." Lana glanced toward the back of the townhouse. "Shouldn't you send more men after the gunman?" *And Trevor?* What if he caught up with the man who'd tried to kill her? If Trevor cornered him, he might try to kill Trevor.

Her pulse kicked up, and she half stood.

The EMT who was taking her blood pressure frowned and held her arm, keeping her from rising all the way to a standing position. "Please. Let the professionals do their jobs."

She bit her lip and settled back on the sofa, tapping her foot as she waited for news about Trevor and the gunman.

What was taking them so long? Had the gunman gotten away? Had he hurt Trevor?

Had it been a mistake sending that text message to Trevor? If anything happened to him, Lana didn't know what she'd do. Though she hadn't seen him in a year, not a day had gone by that she hadn't thought about him.

And every time she thought about Trevor, guilt gripped her heart and squeezed it so hard she could barely breathe. After Mason's death, she'd wanted to fall into Trevor's arms and let him hold her forever. She loved both men. But was clinging to Trevor fair to her deceased husband? At the time, he hadn't been dead for even a week.

What kind of person did that make her, she'd wondered. A selfish, heartless widow. No. She'd decided she couldn't lean on Trevor. It wasn't fair to him, and it wasn't fair to Mason's memory.

So, she'd spoken to Trevor on the phone when he'd called, telling him she was fine when her heart was breaking for so many reasons. She'd lost her husband, whom she'd loved dearly, and she'd lost her best friend because of her sense of guilt.

Now that Trevor was back, Lana wasn't sure she

could push him away again. Hell, she didn't know whether he'd gone on with his life. He could have a girlfriend, a fiancée or a lover.

His promise to Mason to look after her might be the only reason he'd returned.

Lana squared her shoulders. She needed to handle this problem on her own. She never should have texted Trevor.

With that thought came another. If she hadn't contacted him, she would've been dead by now.

CHAPTER 3

TREVOR RACED after the man who'd attempted to murder the only woman he'd ever loved. He wouldn't let him get away. He couldn't allow him to run free and make another attempt on Lana's life.

The metal clang of a trashcan hitting the pavement sounded ahead of him. His muscles straining, Trevor pushed faster. A dark figure rounded the corner of a house, disappearing out of sight.

Trevor focused all his energy on catching up and taking out the man who'd dared to shoot at Lana.

Lifting his elbows and knees, he pushed harder, faster and leaned into the corner, skidding sideways on loose gravel.

Something round and metal swung toward him, blocking his vision a second before it collided with his forehead with a loud bonging sound like a bell or a large cymbal.

Trevor's head snapped back, and his feet flew out from under him. He landed on his back, the air knocked from his lungs, pain reverberating through his skull.

A metal trashcan lid clattered to the pavement beside him, and footsteps raced away into the night.

Rolling to his side, Trevor pushed up to his hands and knees. His head spun. When he tried to stand, the world tilted.

"Have to catch him," Trevor muttered to himself and shook his head to clear his blurred vision.

The movement only made him dizzier. He clutched his head and trained his eyes on the figure in the distance. Or were there two?

He took a step, swayed and tried another.

His head ached, and his eyes still couldn't focus.

No. He couldn't give up now. But then, what if the assailant circled back?

More footsteps sounded behind Trevor. Turning slowly, he spied the two cops who'd come to their assistance and promptly lost their perp.

Trevor pointed in the direction of the man getting away. "He went that way."

When the officers stopped beside him, he jabbed his finger at the air. "Don't stop. He'll get away."

"He's gone," one of the officers said.

With a groan, Trevor turned back in the direction the gunman had run. Like the officer said, the man was gone.

"Damn!" He faced the two officers as they bent over dragging in huge gulps of air. "And who is watching out for Lana? Did you leave her alone?"

The two men shook their heads. "More units arrived as we left the house."

"Did you at least wait until they made certain Lana was okay?"

"She seemed fine," the other officer said.

"Hold one," Officer number one held up a finger and clicked the key on his mic. "How's the homeowner?"

"EMTs are looking at her now," a static-y voice responded.

The cop looked up. "Like I said, she's covered." Still breathing hard, he hooked Trevor's arm. "We'll need you to return to the house."

Trevor jerked his arm free of the officer's hold. "I'm not the shooter."

"I didn't say you were, but we need to ask you questions about what happened."

With a deeply indrawn breath, Trevor nodded. The police officers were only doing their jobs. "Let's head back first, and I'll answer questions along the way, as long as you can keep up."

On the way back to the townhouse, Trevor filled the two officers in on what he'd observed from outside the townhouse and what had happened once he'd climbed up the trellis.

"Have you ever seen this man before?" the officer asked.

"You saw as much as I did. He was wearing a ski mask. I didn't have time to rip it off his head."

"He could be anyone," the shorter officer remarked.

"That's why I was trying to stop him. If he tried to kill Mrs. Connolly once, he might go after her again."

"It could have been a simple break-in."

"The man didn't stop to take anything like electronics or jewelry from the ground level. He headed straight up the stairs and aimed his gun at Mrs. Connolly. If she hadn't been blessed with brains, she'd be a dead woman by now."

Trevor had been half-walking, half-jogging through the alley, eager to get back to Lana and make sure she really was all right. Until he knew for certain, he couldn't calm down and couldn't quite catch his breath.

At the end of the row of townhouses, Trevor veered toward the front of the structure, figuring Lana would be outside on the lawn or in the street answering questions and giving her account of what had happened.

No fewer than six squad cars lined the street, along with an ambulance and a fire truck. Lights flashed, and emergency personnel milled around the street, in the house and on the lawn. Neighboring tenants poked their heads out of their front doors or peered through the windows.

In the middle of them stood Lana and an EMT who was just slapping a bandage on her upper arm. She gave the man a small smile and glanced around at the chaos of flashing lights, deep shadows and people.

When her gaze found him, she pushed away from the first responder and ran toward Trevor.

He opened his arms, and she flung herself into them.

"Oh, Trevor," she sobbed. "I was so worried about you."

He held her, reveling in the feel of her warm curves pressed against his harder planes. God, he'd dreamed of holding her in his arms every night over the past two years. First, after she'd married Mason. And then after Mason had died.

Now he held her in his arms, as he'd always dreamed, and he couldn't tell her how it made him feel.

Lana wasn't his to love. She was his best friend's widow. He'd promised to take care of her and, because of his own selfish longings, he'd failed Lana and Mason miserably.

At that moment, Lana didn't need the messiness of a man who wanted her for his woman. She needed a man who was her friend and protector.

He set her at arm's length and tipped up her chin. "You okay?"

She nodded, tears flooding her eyes, hovering on the rims but stopping short of falling. "I'm okay."

He touched her arm where the EMT had cleaned and bandaged her wound. "He got you?" His jaw clenched. "I should have killed him while I had the chance."

Lana gave a short bark of laughter. "I wish you had, too." She stepped away and rubbed her hands along her arms, her face pale. "I don't know what I would have done if you hadn't shown up when you did."

Trevor's mouth twisted. "You were doing pretty well on your own."

She shook her head. "He would've killed me." Lana shivered and bit her lip as it, too, trembled. "Why did you come?" She looked away. "I told you I'd handle things on my own."

"I stayed away far too long. I promised Connolly I'd look out for you."

"You have," Lana insisted.

Trevor's lips twisted. "A call once a month is not looking out for anyone. I should've been here for you all this time."

Lana shrugged without looking his way. "I've been managing on my own."

"I know you can manage on your own under

normal circumstances. But what happened tonight was anything but normal."

"He was just an intruder. It could have happened to anyone."

"I suspect he knew you'd be alone. And he didn't seem to be there to rob you."

Her gaze swung toward him. "How do you know?"

"He could've stolen anything he wanted on the first floor. You might never have heard him." Trevor closed his eyes as he relived the horror of watching the man heading up the stairs when Lana was alone in her bedroom. He opened his eyes and stared at her. "He was after you."

Lana nodded far too quickly.

Trevor frowned. "You think so, too?"

She nodded and glanced around at the policemen climbing into their vehicles.

The officer in charge stepped up to her. "You can't stay in the bedroom upstairs. It's a crime scene. If you stay here tonight, you'll have to remain on the ground floor. Do you want us to position a uniform in front of your home for the rest of the night?"

Lana shook her head.

"If you don't feel safe here, you might consider staying at a hotel," the policeman suggested.

Again, she shook her head and glanced toward Trevor.

He hooked her arm. "She'll have a friend staying with her."

The cop nodded. "Good. Don't hesitate to call if he comes back."

Lana held up her hand. "Oh, we won't hesitate."

The officers allowed Lana to enter her townhouse and go upstairs long enough to collect what she'd need from her bedroom.

Trevor waited at the door to her bedroom while she gathered clothes and a suitcase. Then he walked with her to the ground floor. "I think you should stay in a hotel tonight."

She shook her head, rubbing her arms with her cool hands. "I don't think it's necessary. I'll be fine here. I can sleep in the spare bedroom down here." Lana faced him. "But you don't have to stay."

"The hell, I don't." Trevor crossed his arms over his chest. "I'm staying." He tilted his head toward the couch. "I'll be comfortable on the couch."

"My couch is small. Your body's much longer than that couch will hold."

He snorted. "I've slept under much worse conditions."

Her lips pressed into a thin line. "Yeah, but you don't need to be uncomfortable now. You're not in a war zone."

"I'm not in a war zone when I go to my mother's house, but she insists on keeping my old bunkbed from when I was a kid."

Lana snorted, a smile tugging at her lips. "I can picture you lying in a child's bed with your legs hanging over the end."

His heart warmed at the brief smile on her face. This was the Lana he remembered from when the three of them had been such great friends. She'd had such a zest for life, her eyes always dancing with mischief. Her joy was the reason he'd fallen in love with Lana in the first place.

And why he was still very much in love with her.

Keeping his relationship with Lana impersonal would be hell. But he couldn't desert her now.

Lana shot a skeptical glance toward the couch. She frowned. "You could sleep on the guest bed, and I can take the—"

"I'll sleep on the couch," he said, his voice stern. "If you want to help, a pillow would be nice."

She gave a quick nod. "I can do that." Lana spun, ran into the guest bedroom and returned carrying a pillow with a cotton-candy pink pillowcase.

When she handed him the pillow, their hands touched, and an electric shock zipped up Trevor's arm and into his chest.

He snatched the pillow and backed a step away, his gaze rising to hers.

Her eyes had widened, and her mouth formed a soft O. Just as quickly, she clamped her mouth shut, lowered her glance and looked toward the damaged door of the townhouse. "Did you need anything from your vehicle? I have an extra toothbrush, soap and shampoo, if you want it. There's a small shower in the guest bedroom on this level. The place isn't very big, but it's comfortable. Are you hungry? Do you need an extra blanket?" She gave him a sheepish smile. "I'm sorry. I talk too much when I'm—you know."

"When you're nervous." He gave her a sad smile. "You were never nervous around me when we were The Three Musketeers."

She shrugged. "That was a long time ago. Things changed."

He nodded. "Yes. They did. You chose the right guy. Mason was perfect husband material."

Her eyes glazed, and she bit down on her bottom lip. She glanced away and paused for a moment before saying, "You must be exhausted. Did you fly in from Montana today?"

He shook his head. "I'm fine. And yes, I flew down this evening."

"I sent you that text earlier today. How did you get a flight so quickly?" She held up her hands. "Not that I'm complaining. I don't know what I'd have done without you." Tears slipped down her cheeks.

Trevor's chest tightened. He never could stand to see Lana cry. He opened his arms. "You knew I'd come."

She walked into his embrace and rested her cheek against his shirt. "Thank you for being here."

He held her again, careful not to breathe too deeply and make his chest press too tightly against hers. He could like this far too much and be just as heartbroken as he'd been when he'd discovered she'd said yes to Mason.

He still had the ring he'd planned to propose with. Perhaps in the back of his mind, he'd hoped that someday he'd have a second shot at getting it right. How pathetic was that?

Trevor reminded himself that she'd chosen Connolly and poaching on a dead man's widow just wasn't right. He pushed her to arm's length. "I'd like to get a shower, and then we need to talk."

She nodded.

He checked the back door, making certain the deadbolt was in place and he jammed a chair beneath the handle of the front door the cops had damaged. Then he grabbed her hand and started for the downstairs bathroom. "You're coming with me."

"Into the shower?" she squeaked and dug her feet into the floor.

He forced himself to laugh. "No, but into the bedroom with the door locked. If someone tries to get in, you can let me know before anything bad happens. I'll leave the bathroom door cracked open."

"Oh. Okay." Her cheeks burned a bright red, and she hurried ahead of him to the bedroom. On the threshold, she halted and pressed a hand to her chest.

Trevor touched a hand to the small of her back

and glanced over her shoulder into the room. "What's wrong?"

"It's just…" She sighed. "I've never had someone shoot at me before. And in my own bedroom."

"Something about bringing it too close to home?" he asked softly.

Lana nodded. "Makes me feel like there's nowhere safe, now."

He wanted to pull her into his arms and hug away her fears. Instead, he draped his arm over her shoulders. "I'm here with you. I won't let anything happen to you."

She smiled up at him. "That helps." Still, she hesitated.

"Let me do a sweep of the room. Maybe that will set your mind at ease." He slipped past her into the bedroom and checked the closet, under the bed and glanced through the window. "Sorry I had to break your window upstairs. I'll clean up the glass once it's not cordoned off."

"I'm not worried about the glass. It can be replaced." Lana entered the room and looked around at the neatly made bed. "The question is, how did you get up to my window in the first place?" She stopped in front of the downstairs bedroom window.

"I climbed the trellis." He frowned. "If you plan on staying here, you might consider having it taken down. It's too easy for a burglar to get into your place." He touched her shoulder. "You also might not want to stand in front of the window. If someone wanted to shoot you, you're presenting an easy target."

Lana ducked back behind the wall. "On second thought, I don't think I can stay here." She waved at the window. "He came through the kitchen window, you came through the upstairs window. Who's to say he won't break into this one?" She shook her head. "I just can't."

Trevor nodded. "I understand. Grab your bag. I'll take you to a hotel." When they got there, he'd either get a suite or share the room with her. He wasn't letting her too far out of his sight.

CHAPTER 4

LANA GRABBED the small suitcase in which she'd packed several days' worth of clothing. She'd grabbed and stuffed panties, bras, shirts, trousers and jeans, not knowing when she'd be back in her townhouse or where she was going to stay. After a quick glance around for anything else she might need from the living room, she went in search of Trevor. She found him in the kitchen, staring at the broken glass on the floor.

"I'm ready," she said.

"I feel bad about leaving the mess I made upstairs. I'll clean it up, when we come back" he insisted.

Picturing him performing such domestic duties made Lana smile. "You saved my ass. Cleaning up a little glass is the least I could do to repay you."

"No repayment necessary. Anyone would have done the same."

Lana snorted. "Not hardly. I don't know many grown men who'd scale a rickety trellis to a woman's window, and then break the window with his elbow." She frowned. "Speaking of which... Let me check you over. You probably have cuts."

"Surprisingly, I don't. A couple scratches, maybe, but no real bleeders. We need to leave, if we're not staying. Now that the police are gone, the longer we hang out here, the more chance the intruder could circle back and make another attempt."

Lana's heart skipped several beats, and a lead weight settled in the pit of her belly. "You think he'll come back tonight?"

"Do you want to take the risk? I'd rather get a head start and find a hotel without a tail following us."

When he put it that way, leaving her home didn't seem like such a bad idea. She squared her shoulders. "I'm packed."

Trevor raised an eyebrow at her one suitcase. "That's all you're bringing?"

"It's enough for a week. If I need anything else, I'll find a place to do laundry." She headed for the bedroom door. "I'll call the facilities manager in the morning and have them board up the window until the glass can be replaced and do something about the damaged door."

"Let me go first." Trevor led the way down the

47

stairs and to the front door of the apartment, where he stopped and pointed a finger at her chest. "Stay."

Her lips twisted. "You make me sound like a dog. But I'll stay put, as you've requested."

"And jam the chair beneath the door handle behind me. I'm going to secure the perimeter." He left through the front door and disappeared into the shadows.

Lana closed the door and pushed the chair beneath the handle, her pulse hammering, her ears perked for any sound beyond the wood paneling.

She prayed Trevor didn't run into any problems while out checking for bad guys. Lana had to remind herself that he was a trained Navy SEAL. He had to have performed more than one urban operation going from building to building with a loaded weapon, facing the possibility of running into enemy fighters also possessing loaded guns. What he was doing out there was no different than what he might have done on foreign soil. He knew what to do and how to stay as safe as possible.

Knowing all that didn't make her pulse beat any slower. She held her breath until a light tap on the door made her jump. She peered through the peephole to find Trevor grinning on the other side.

"It's me," he said.

She removed the chair and yanked open the door, her heart beating fast. "I thought you'd never come back."

He stepped inside, closed the door behind him and pulled her into his arms. "You know me better. I'd come back if at all humanly possible."

She pressed her forehead into his shirt. "That part about being 'humanly possible' was what had me worried."

He held her for a moment longer, and then gripped her shoulders and leaned back. "Ready?"

No. She wasn't ready, but she nodded anyway.

"Stay close to me," he said, then opened the door and led the way outside.

She started toward her car.

He gripped her elbow and steered her away. "If you don't mind, I'd rather take the rental car."

"But you wouldn't have to pay for extra days on your car if we take mine," she insisted.

"Yeah, but if someone tried to kill you by shooting you, I wouldn't put it past him to tamper with your car."

She swallowed hard, fear settling on her shoulders like a heavy weight. "Surely, he wouldn't have had time to do that."

"If it's all the same to you, I don't want to test the theory." He led her toward his rental car and settled her into the passenger seat.

She watched as he checked over the entire vehicle for any tampering or explosive devices. Then he rounded the front of the vehicle, his gaze sweeping the parking lot.

Lana reminded herself he was a professionally-trained operative. Whatever he said would go.

Trevor slid into the driver's seat and started the engine. After a quick check all around, he pulled out of the parking lot and onto the road.

"Where are we going?" Lana asked.

"Right now, I don't know." He checked the rearview mirror and the side mirrors. "I want to get as far away from your townhouse as possible. What I need you to do is check to make sure no one is following us. Got that?"

She nodded.

"When we're sure we're on our own, we'll look for a place to stay." He shot a glance toward her. "Are you okay with this?"

She twisted her lips. "Do I have a choice?"

He shrugged. "Not really. I'm going to do whatever I think is necessary to keep you safe. I can only hope you'll go along with what I suggest. It's up to you."

"Oh, I didn't mean that I minded you giving the orders. I meant, do I have choice about being followed." She raised her hands. "Trust me. I'll do whatever you think is best." She adjusted her seatbelt and turned sideways in the seat to look behind them. "It shouldn't be hard to see if someone is following us. Their headlights will be a dead giveaway."

"If they're using headlights." Trevor waved toward

the streetlights. "They could be driving without them."

Lana nodded. "Got it. Look for anything that looks like it's following us. Lights or not."

Trevor chuckled. "That's my girl."

Lana's heart warmed at the sound of Trevor's laughter. She missed the old days when she, Mason and Trevor hung out at the team's favorite watering hole. They'd been so close.

Until Mason had asked her to marry him, and she'd said yes. She'd been closing in on twenty-six years old. All her friends had already been married, with one baby and another on the way. Meanwhile, Lana had still been living the single life, but she'd started to feel her biological clock ticking.

She'd thought about marriage but had loved both Mason and Trevor and couldn't decide between them.

She'd kissed Trevor once and had felt all kinds of sparks when they had. But then she'd kissed Mason twice and felt the same.

When Mason had taken her out on a real date, just the two of them, and ended the evening asking her to marry him, saying yes had come so naturally.

What had started as an incredibly close friendship between the three of them, fell quickly apart the moment Lana had agreed to marry Mason.

She didn't know why, but she'd assumed they'd all remain friends, even after she married Mason. But that hadn't quite happened. Yes, Trevor had still cared about Mason as a friend and teammate, and he'd said he cared about her, but he'd stopped hanging out with them. He'd said he was giving them the space they needed as a couple.

Trevor had been Mason's best man at their wedding. He'd smiled and congratulated them along with the rest of their friends and teammates. He'd even kissed the bride...on the forehead...and then he'd taken a quick step backward, letting others come up to congratulate the new couple.

When Mason died, Trevor told Lana he'd promised Mason he'd take care of her.

Lana had been upset by her husband's death and her own desire to lean heavily on Trevor. Grief and guilt had torn a hole in her heart. The only other human she'd loved as much as her husband had been Trevor. But she hadn't felt right going to him when she could so easily have married Trevor instead of Mason.

If Trevor had asked.

Now, she felt as though she'd been given a second chance with Trevor. What did that make her? What wife could love another man so soon after her own husband's death? But then Lana had loved both men.

She'd felt guilty that she'd wanted Trevor after her husband's death. So guilty that she'd pushed the man away. She'd wanted to prove to herself she could get on with life, without a man to lean on. To prove to herself, and to Mason's spirit, that she'd truly loved him. She owed it to her husband to figure out why he'd died.

The medical report of his injuries indicated he'd been shot in the back. When she'd questioned the report, she'd been given a less than adequate response. Based on his last communication with her, she suspected someone hadn't wanted him to learn more about crooked Americans working deals in Afghanistan. So much so, that they'd been willing to kill to keep their secrets.

After his death, she'd had enough money from Mason's life insurance that she hadn't immediately gone back to work. Instead, she'd spent time on her computer, researching the US companies working reconstruction projects and protective services. She'd learned a lot, but not as much as she'd learned once she'd hooked up with a hacker on the dark web. He'd gotten her into databases for some of those companies and recovered email records of their people with boots on the ground on the other side of the world.

Lana's dark web hacker had found links between the director at the Department of Homeland Security in San Diego and one of the general contractors working in Afghanistan when Mason was killed.

Based on that information, Lana had applied for an advertised position at the DHS, working for one of the people her quest had led her to find.

Thankfully, she'd become friends with Peter

Bishop at the DHS. She hadn't told him about her connection with the man working on the dark web. When Peter had caught her looking into files she shouldn't have been accessing, she'd told him she suspected someone was plotting terrorist activities on homeland soil.

Peter had been so concerned he'd offered to help her find the person. Her new friend had done some sleuthing on his own, following the director and staking out some of his favorite haunts, taking pictures and recording the dates and times the man met with different people.

He'd also tapped into the director's personal email and home computer IP address and found connections to other potentially dangerous organizations.

Still, the evidence didn't seem to be enough to convict the director. Peter said he was at a standstill on his personal investigation and wasn't sure he wanted to continue digging.

Lana understood. For the past year, the effort had consumed her to the point she wasn't engaged in anything other than going to work during the day and searching the internet at night.

Early that morning, Lana had received a missive from her dark web contact. He'd found more connections to a group based in the Bitterroot Mountains of Montana that had posted negative comments about the current US administration, promising to take back the America they once knew and loved.

He'd given her the names of two of the people living in a small town in the mountains of Montana.

That was when Lana knew she was getting in over her head, and it was time to let the FBI take over. She'd gathered the data on her computer into one file, backed it up on the cloud and set up the meeting with the FBI for the following day.

She'd gone to work as usual, but she hadn't felt comfortable, worrying that she was being watched all the time. Which was ridiculous. The only other person, besides the dark web contact, who knew she was looking into a possible terrorist attack was Peter.

And he'd come by her desk smiling and had greeted her as if nothing strange was going on with the director or anything else.

"Lana, sweetheart." Trevor's voice pulled her out of her reverie and back to their current situation. "We have a tail."

She lifted her head and focused on the headlights behind them. Her pulse leaped. If she wasn't mistaken, the vehicle was catching up to them.

Fast.

"I think they're going to—"

Bam! The vehicle behind them slammed into the back of the rental car.

Lana jerked forward. The seatbelt across her

shoulder dug in hard, keeping her from hitting her head on the dashboard.

When she sat upright, she spun to see the car behind them race at them for a second time. "Hold on. Here he comes again."

TREVOR'S GRIP on the steering wheel couldn't be tighter. With his foot on the accelerator all the way to the floor, he couldn't go any faster.

The vehicle behind them rammed into them again.

The car lurched forward and skidded a little to the side. Tires gripped the pavement, gaining enough traction to shoot them forward.

They couldn't outrun the attacker. Next best thing would be to avoid him.

After regaining control of the vehicle, Trevor turned the wheel sharply to the right, aiming for the next street corner.

The back end of the car fishtailed, whipping out behind them, sending them into a one-hundred-eighty-degree spin. Now, they faced the vehicle that had hit them.

"Damn! Hold tight," Trevor yelled as the other car raced straight at them.

Trevor pressed his foot on the gas and aimed for the oncoming vehicle.

"What are you doing?" Lana held onto the armrest

with one hand and threw her arm up over her face with the other.

At the last minute before hitting the attacking vehicle head on, Trevor jerked the wheel to the right and gave it all the gas. He missed the head-on collision, but the vehicle clipped the back bumper, sending him into a full-out spin.

Trevor turned the steering wheel into the spin and rode it out until the car slowed enough he could regain control. Thankfully, he was headed the opposite direction of the vehicle that had hit them. He put the pedal to the metal and raced away.

"He's turning around," Lana said.

A glance in the rearview mirror confirmed her observation. "We're not going to let him get to us this time," Trevor promised. He took the first right turn, raced to the next block and made a left. At the next block, he made another right turn.

Zigzagging through the streets of San Diego, he climbed up hills and zipped down a couple of dark alleys.

Lana sat sideways in the seat, looking back. "I think you lost him," she said finally and turned to face him. "Good job getting us out of there. I hope you had full insurance coverage on the rental car. I'm sure the damage is going to take some explaining."

"I don't give a damn about the car." He shot a glance toward Lana. "Are you all right?"

She rubbed a hand across her neck. "Other than a sore neck, I'll live. How about you?"

"I'm fine. But this situation has me concerned about your safety."

She snorted softly. "You and me both."

After another glance in the rearview mirror, reassuring him they weren't being followed this time, he said, "Let's find a hotel room and get some sleep. Then tomorrow we can decide what we do next."

"There's no question about what I need to do." She stared ahead at the dark road, lit by an occasional street light. "I have an appointment with the FBI."

"About that, you need to fill me in on why you're meeting with the FBI and what you know that has someone out to kill you."

"That could take a while."

He smiled, staring at the quiet city street in front of him. "I have all night. Lay it on me."

"I'll fill you in on all the details when we get to the hotel." She twisted her hands in her lap, a frown denting her forehead. "I should have called you earlier. I'm in way over my head."

The neon light of a small motel glowed like a beacon in the night. It looked old, but the grounds were well-maintained, and it had a retro feel to it. Trevor pulled in. Tired to the bone and in need of a couple hours of shut-eye, he still looked around for signs of potential threats.

Lana chewed on her bottom lip as she stared at

the two-story building. Only a handful of cars were parked in the parking lot. "Are you sure we'll be safe in a motel?"

"I'll park the car behind the building. No one will know we're here unless they drive around the structure."

Lana nodded and gripped the door handle.

"Stay here, while I get a room."

Trevor parked in front of the motel's office and walked up to the bullet-proof glass window. He cringed. Bullet-proof glass didn't bode well for the establishment, but going to a more populated, well-lit area put them at too much risk. As long as the room was clean, and they could hide the car in back, they could deal with one night.

The man behind the counter had dark skin and dark, straight hair. He appeared to be eating food from a Styrofoam container. He laid down his fork and approached the window, his eyes narrowing. "May I help you?"

"My...wife and I need a room for the night." Trevor stood sideways to the clerk, his attention divided between the office and the car where Lana sat patiently waiting.

"We have several rooms to choose from," the man said in a stilted British accent. "Upstairs or down?"

"We prefer the privacy at the back of the building. Downstairs."

The motel clerk checked his computer screen.

"The second room from the end is available. One key or two?"

"One, please." Lana had to understand they couldn't be split up into two different rooms. He had to be as close as possible to keep her safe.

"And I'll need a toothbrush, if you have one."

The clerk nodded and quoted a dollar amount.

Trevor opened his wallet and extracted enough cash, not even considering leaving his credit card. If the attacker figured out who he was, he could potentially trace him through his credit cards. Having rammed the back of the rental vehicle, he could easily have gotten the license plate and could learn who he was by tracing him through the rental agreement. Using cash was the only way to stay off the grid until they got away from San Diego. And California.

The idea of leaving California took root in Trevor's mind. If he could get her out of the city and to a place where he could see the enemy coming...a place like the wide-open spaces of Montana...he had a better chance of keeping her safe.

As soon as they settled in the room, he'd bring up the subject. But first, he had to stash the car and get her into the room. The single room, where both of them would sleep for what was left of the night.

His groin tightened.

He'd given up on having Lana as his own when she'd agreed to marry Mason. But that decision didn't begin to quell the way his body reacted to her. He still wanted her...still loved her. With Mason gone, would it be so wrong to pursue her and make her his?

The image of Connolly dying in his arms forced Trevor to give himself a firm shake. Lana was his friend's widow. He'd promised to look out for her, not to jump her bones and make love to her after he was in the ground. A year still seemed like yesterday to Trevor. A year in which he hadn't seen Lana and had only spoken on the phone with her once a month.

He'd thought staying away would lessen the desire and longing he had for the only woman he'd ever loved. If anything, it had strengthened his yearning. He hadn't dated any women since he'd met Lana. He'd thought about it and had almost asked one of the waitresses from the Blue Moon Tavern in Eagle Rock, Montana to go out with him. However, before he could open his mouth to pose the question, images of Lana rose in his memory, and he couldn't do it. Lana was the girl for him. No one came close to competing.

But Lana was hands-off. He couldn't remind himself enough.

Squaring his shoulders, he tucked the toothbrush the clerk handed to him into his pocket and turned toward the car. Lana sat staring through the window. Though the reason for his visit was unsettling, the joy of seeing her there couldn't be denied. He drew in a deep breath, marched to the car, slid into the driver's seat and cranked the engine.

"Did you get us rooms?" Lana's husky voice melted like butter over every pore of Trevor's skin. His jeans tightened, and he tossed the room key into her lap.

"Room," he corrected. "I got us a room."

"Not adjoining rooms?"

He shook his head. "I don't want you out of my sight, except when you're in the bathroom."

"I'd say you were taking it a little too far, but..." she shivered, "you're probably right. I can sleep in one of the chairs."

"I'll sleep sitting up. I don't want to be surprised."

"You're too big a guy to sit up in a chair all night."

"It's only be a couple hours until morning. I've had less sleep on a mission."

"And I'm a mission?" She shook her head. "You're not as young as you used to be, and we both need sleep to keep up our energy reserves." She crossed her arms over her chest. "I'll take a shift for a couple hours while you sleep."

He shot a look her way, a smile tugging at the corners of his lips. "You're still as stubborn as I remember."

Her mouth firmed into a straight line. "Damn right. And don't you forget it."

"Yes, ma'am." Trevor parked the car behind the

building. No part of the vehicle would be visible from the main road. Unless someone drove into the parking lot and around to the back of the motel, the car wouldn't be seen.

Trevor slipped out of the driver's seat and rounded the front of the sedan.

Before he reached the door, Lana was out and standing on the pavement, the key in her hand. She turned toward the rear of the vehicle where they'd stashed her suitcase.

"Leave it," Trevor said. "I'll get it when you're safely inside."

"I can do some things for myself, you know," she muttered.

"I know. Just humor me."

She stiffened. "I will, but don't get crazy on doing everything for me. I like my independence, in case you didn't remember that about me."

He touched a hand to the small of her back. "Oh, I remember, all right. You always were a law unto yourself. You made your own decisions."

Some of the starch left her spine. "Yeah, I make my own decisions." Her lips closed together in a tight line as she marched toward the door.

The key slid into the lock without any trouble.

Lana turned it and the knob at once, and the door opened.

Before she could step inside, Trevor touched her shoulder. "Let me go first."

She frowned. "Afraid there's someone waiting inside to jump me?"

"No, but there might be bugs. And I remember how you felt about roaches."

She shivered and grimaced. "Right, again. I can deal with snakes, attackers and rude people. But cockroaches make me lose it." She waved him past her. "By all means, go first."

Again, she shivered. "Now, I won't sleep at all. I'll see images of bugs crawling over me for the rest of the night."

"Don't borrow trouble," Trevor warned. "And don't stand beneath a street light. We don't want anyone to identify you."

Lana pulled back her shoulders and stuck out her chest. With a mock salute, she said, "Okay, let's get inside."

Trevor made a quick sweep of the room, checking for bad guys and bugs. He also checked the bed linens. The room was dated, the furnishings old, but it was clean, and the sheets appeared to be freshly laundered.

He returned to the door. "It's safe to enter."

"No bad guys," Lana asked.

Trevor shook his head.

"No bugs?" Lana quizzed.

"None that I saw," Trevor replied.

"Great. Let me look." She pushed past him into the room, her gaze roving the floor, the walls and into the bathroom. When she emerged, her eyes were narrowed. "You're right. None that I can see." She pulled back the bedspread and pillows. "They look clean enough. I suppose it'll do."

Trevor flipped the deadbolt and secured the chain over the door. They were locked in for the night. He turned to face Lana. "Now that we've conducted a thorough investigation, do you want to shower first?"

"I'll shower in the morning. It helps me wake up and gives my hair a fighting chance for a style." She lifted her arms toward the ceiling. "Right now, I need sleep."

"You have the bed. I'm hitting the shower. I didn't have a chance to shower and change before I hopped on board a plane to get here."

Her brow furrowed. "I'm sorry my message was so cryptic. As soon as I sent it, I wished I could retract the text."

"I'm glad you couldn't. And I'm glad I made it here in time."

She nodded. "Me, too."

An awkward silence fell over the room.

After their years of friendship, Trevor regretted that silence. They used to be able to say anything to each other. "Lana—"

She held up her hand, her eyes glistening in the limited light glowing from the sconce attached to the wall over the nightstand. "Get your shower. We can talk afterward."

He wanted to clear the air first, but the look on her face, as though she was struggling with herself, decided for him. "I'll get our things from the car."

She nodded and turned away.

Using every bit of his strength and resolve, Trevor forced himself to walk out the door and back to the car, when what he wanted to do was take Lana in his arms and reassure her everything would be all right.

But he wasn't sure everything would be all right. He didn't know who was after her. More importantly, he didn't know where he stood in her life. She'd pushed him away after Mason's death. Was she as determined to expel him from her life after the dust settled on her current situation?

CHAPTER 5

AFTER TREVOR LEFT THE ROOM, Lana stared at the wall for a long moment, fighting to keep from doing what she wanted to do most. She wanted to fall into the man's arms and let him hold her until all the bad left her life.

But part of the bad had to do with the loss of Mason. That situation wasn't going away. Mason and Trevor had been the best of friends, until she'd chosen to marry Mason.

The key turned in the lock, and the door opened behind her.

She glanced over her shoulder.

Trevor entered, carrying her suitcase.

"Did you bring anything from Montana?" she asked.

"I didn't have time to go by the B&B I'm staying at there. I went straight to the airport."

ELLE JAMES

Her lips twitched. Trevor had always been there for Mason and herself. Even after she'd married Mason, whenever Mason had called for help moving something heavy, Trevor had been there.

He set the bag on the bed.

"Do you need any toiletries?" she asked. "I have shampoo and conditioner and an extra tube of toothpaste."

Trevor patted his front shirt pocket. "I have a toothbrush, and I think I saw soap and trial-sized bottles of shampoo in the bathroom. I'm set."

She nodded, her heart skipping several beats as she watched Trevor stride toward the bathroom. He wore his softly faded jeans well, the back pocket cupping his ass to perfection.

Heat built inside Lana.

Trevor paused at the door. "You know the drill."

She nodded. "Don't open the door. If anyone tries to get in, I get you out of the shower."

"Right." He winked, entered the bathroom and closed the door halfway.

Lana opened her suitcase and selected a T-shirt and leggings from the pile of clothing she'd stuffed inside. Her gaze darted to the half-open doorway.

Trevor pulled his T-shirt up his chest and over his head. He tossed it into the sink, filled the sink with water and a squirt of shampoo, and washed the shirt.

It hit Lana again. The man had come straight from Montana to help her. What had he left behind?

Did he have a girlfriend? After a year away, he had every right to get on with his life. And the man was amazing to look at. She stared at his profile, admiring massive shoulders and the muscles rippling down his back. He could have any woman he wanted at the snap of his fingers.

For a moment, Lana wondered how she would respond if Trevor snapped his fingers and told her to join him in the shower.

Deep down, she knew.

She'd join him in the shower. Regrets and self-loathing would come later. But for a few brief moments, sliding her naked body against his would be pure heaven.

Heat coiled low in her belly, and she ached for the first time since her husband's death. Ached for a man's touch. Not just any man. She loved Trevor. But that ship had sailed when she'd chosen to marry Mason. And her love for Mason had been just as strong.

How could one woman love two men? But she had. Still, she wasn't the kind of woman who could marry two men. Mason and Trevor were alpha men, through and through. They would never have shared her between them. As a friend, yes. As a wife. No way.

And the two men lived by the code: you don't mess with another man's wife. Especially a man who is your best friend.

Trevor had lived up to that code, though his friendship with Mason had been somewhat strained up to the wedding and even after they'd exchanged vows.

Though Lana had been happily married to Mason, she'd always felt like a traitor to Trevor. Now that Mason was dead, she couldn't seduce the man. Not after she'd ditched him to marry his best friend.

It didn't matter that she'd wanted what other women had. A man to come home to. Babies, when they were ready for them. A home in the suburbs where their children could play in a nice yard.

Way back when she, Mason and Trevor started hanging out, Trevor had been adamant about not wanting to get married. He had too much life to live, and marriage would slow him down.

But then he'd kissed her... *Dear Lord.* That kiss had been electric. To her, at least. He hadn't tried to kiss her again, nor had he said anything about it. So likely, it hadn't been as monumental for him.

Then Mason had taken her out on an honest-to-God date, ending it with a proposal of marriage that had completely shocked her and made her happy at the same time.

She'd loved Mason. She'd loved Trevor. Of the two men, Mason had seemed the safest choice. He'd never said he didn't want to get married, and she'd known he would make a wonderful father to their children.

Lana had said yes. She'd never regretted marrying Mason. If anything, she regretted they'd never had a chance at a longer life together.

Now that he was gone, her life stretched before her, a long and empty space. Her chest hurt just thinking about it. And she didn't have children to fill her days or share her love.

She glanced at the bathroom again, just in time to see Trevor shuck his jeans.

She caught a glimpse of long, thickly muscled legs and a tight ass.

Her core coiled into a tight, needy ball. A year of celibacy was wearing on her. But she couldn't come on to Trevor. He'd been Mason's best friend. Lana was sure it would make him incredibly uncomfortable. And it would fill her with that same guilt she'd felt when he'd held her in his arms after the funeral.

Torn between wanting the man, and doing right by her dead husband, Lana forced herself to turn away.

The squeak of the shower curtain rings sliding across the bar and the water turning on made her imagine Trevor standing there naked, water rivulets trickling down the front of his broad chest.

Even looking away didn't help to keep her body's response under control.

She wanted to seduce Trevor and claim him. The urge to strip down to her birthday suit and join him in the shower was so strong she was afraid to move lest she do just that.

For a long moment, she concentrated on breathing in and out, until her pulse calmed, and the insane urge went away.

While Trevor showered, Lana changed into her soft jersey T-shirt and Capri leggings. She'd opted not to take up space in her suitcase for pajamas, knowing she might not get back to her house for a while. She could sleep in the tee and leggings or wear them to a gym, if she wanted to work out. And the best part was that there was nothing sexy about what she was wearing.

She wasn't trying to excite her protector. Not that she could, even in sexy lingerie. He was an honorable man, who would never do anything untoward with respect to his best friend's widow.

The devil on Lana's shoulder wished he would try something.

The water shut off.

Lana pressed her palms to her hot cheeks. She had at least a minute to get a grip before Trevor emerged from the bathroom. She slammed shut her suitcase and shoved it into a corner.

"What was that?" Trevor asked from the open bathroom door.

Lana spun to face him, and her mouth dropped open.

He stood there, wearing nothing but a towel

wrapped low around his hips. The terrycloth formed a bit of tent. The more she stared at the tent, the more it jutted out.

"Are you all right?" Trevor asked. "I thought I heard a gunshot."

"Gunshot?" Lana said, her voice breathy. "Uh. No. Just me shutting my suitcase." She waved a hand nervously. "Shouldn't you put on some clothes?"

"I would, but what I brought with me had to be washed and is hanging up to dry on the curtain rod."

Oh great. She had the hots for her husband's best friend, and that best friend only had a towel to wear through the night.

Her naked roommate would be hell to resist when every cell in Lana's body screamed hallelujah.

"I'll take first shift staying awake if you want to get under the covers and sleep," she offered. *And cover your body from head to toe to keep me from drooling like a groupie.*

She didn't add that last bit, but she thought it. Keeping her mouth shut on what was going on in her head was a real challenge, especially when Trevor emerged in the towel and nothing else.

Lana must have stared too long, because Trevor's brows dipped. "If I make you uncomfortable, I can stay in the bathroom a little longer."

"No." Lana pinched the bridge of her nose. "So, am I taking first shift?"

"If you'd like. I doubt I'll sleep, anyway. We could

talk, and you could tell me why you think you're being targeted."

"Right." She'd completely forgotten she hadn't filled him on all that had happened in the past year. But then all those muscles on display made her forget her own name.

She turned her back to him and started from when she'd learned more about Mason's death.

"He was shot in the back?" Trevor gripped her shoulder and spun her to face him. "Who told you that?"

Her wits scrambled at the clean, fresh scent of Trevor standing in front of her, inches away. Certainly, close enough she could lick him.

She reined in her thoughts. "I spoke with the doctor who declared him dead. He'd made notes about Mason's injuries. That, plus what Mason had told me about his last mission, made me curious enough to dig a little deeper."

"I wish you'd told me about this. I could have helped. I thought the mission was an ambush, and Connolly was collateral damage."

"I think he was collateral damage. But I also think it was initiated from supposedly friendly forces."

"You don't think a member of our own team shot him in the back, do you?" Trevor shook his head. "Everyone we were with that night would have laid down his life to save Connolly, including me."

Lana touched Trevor's chest, eager to make him

understand. A shock of awareness ripped through her and she jerked her hand back. "I believe that. But someone else knew you were out there. Someone who came in from behind. And the bullet they pulled from Mason was one of our own."

"We supply the Afghan forces with the weapons and ammunition they need to defend themselves."

"What about the contractors and the contracted security teams?"

"They have access to the same weapons and ammunition sales. They could have had the same ammunition that's issued to our troops."

"Exactly." She explained how she'd tracked through the contractor data and followed the trail back to San Diego and the regional office of the Department of Homeland Security with the help of her guy on the dark web.

Trevor shook his head, a frown deeply etched across his forehead. "Terrorists, American traitors and the dark web? Where was I through all this?"

"You were in Montana, where you needed to be to get on with your life. This was my project to work. I wanted to know all there was to know about Mason's death."

"But the dark web? Terrorists? At what point did you realize you were wading into dangerous waters?"

She gave him a sheepish grimace. "Today." Lana snorted. "Make that yesterday. It's past midnight. Anyway, that's when I decided to take it to the FBI. I made an appointment to meet with them today. I want to get there, hand off what I know and let them take it from here."

"And that's when you were attacked." Again, Trevor shook his head. "Who else knew you were meeting with the FBI?"

"No one. I made the call on my own cell phone."

"Were you at your office?"

"No. I had just stepped out of the building to go to lunch. I made the call while sitting in my car."

"Are you sure no one overheard your conversation?"

"As sure as I can be."

"Without access to your car, I can't know whether your car was bugged. But that brings up another question. Is your phone being tracked?"

She frowned. "I don't think so."

"When we left your townhouse, we weren't being followed. Ten minutes into our drive, a car appears out of nowhere and rams into the back of ours." Trevor strode toward the bathroom. "Pack your suitcase," he said over his shoulder.

"Where are we going?"

"Anywhere but here." He entered the bathroom, whipped off the towel, grumbling as he went. "I can't believe it took me this long to figure that out."

"Figure out what?" Lana asked, her gaze on his naked backside, her pulse pounding as she lifted her case onto the bed.

"That either you or your phone is being tracked." He shoved his feet into his wet jeans one at a time and tugged them on. As he worked the wet Demin up over his thighs, the muscles of his glutinous maximus flexed. "Do you have something on you that you always bring with you? A purse, a piece of jewelry, anything you carry on a regular basis besides your smart phone?"

Lana dragged her attention away from Trevor's ass. She conducted an inventory of her person and the backpack she'd opted to bring, instead of her purse. "No. Just my cell phone."

"Give it to me." He flung his T-shirt over his head and slicked it down his body, the damp shirt clinging to him like a second skin. Then he held out his hand.

Lana dug her cell phone out of her backpack. "But I need that phone. I took a couple days off, but what if work calls me?"

"They'll do fine without you for a couple of days." He held out his hands and wiggled his fingers. "Give."

She slapped her cell phone into his hand and set her case on the ground. "I'm ready when you are."

"Leave this here," he ordered and set the phone on the dresser. "Now, I'm first out of here. Wait for me."

"I'm not going anywhere, until you tell me to," she replied.

"And stay clear of the door until I come for you."

"Yes, sir."

He rested his hand on the doorknob and gave a

count of three. Then he ripped open the door and stepped outside.

Lana held her breath.

TREVOR PULLED the door closed behind him, immediately stepped to the side and crouched. Why hadn't he thought of her cellphone being tracked before now? Hell, they could have been attacked while he'd been taking his shower.

Something hit the wooden doorframe, sending splinters flying down over him.

Fuck! He'd been shot at, and whoever was doing the shooting had a silencer, making the assailant harder to locate in the dark. With nothing but the direction of the bullet to go on, Trevor ducked behind one of the three vehicles parked in the lot. Hunkering low, he ran the length of the car and dropped to his belly. He inched forward and stared out into the night.

On the other side of the parking lot was a dilapidated chain-link fence with branches of bushes growing through the links. At one point the fence had fallen, taking a portion of the bushes with it. The position was almost directly across from the room he and Lana occupied.

Getting to that position meant crossing the parking lot, which would be the fastest route. Or he'd have to backtrack and swing toward the back of the building, jump the fence and go around behind the bushes.

Or…he had one more idea.

Backing behind the vehicle, he judged the distance between the car and the corner of the building. On the count of three, he took off running, staying low to the ground and zig-zagging to keep from being an easy target.

Bullets pinged off the pavement around him, but he kept running and dove around the corner.

Trevor rolled to his feet, dug his keys from his wet pocket and unlocked the rental car's doors.

He got in and started the engine. Knowing they might have to make a swift escape, he'd backed into the parking space. Now, he shifted into drive and tore around the corner and straight for the downed fence and gap in the bushes.

He ducked low as a barrage of bullets hit the windshield where his head had been. The front of the vehicle plowed into the broken fence and the equally damaged bush.

A dark figure rolled out of the bushes, onto his feet and ran toward a dark SUV in an abandoned parking lot on the other side of the fence.

Trevor whipped the car into reverse, backed up to the motel room where Lana waited and jumped out.

He pounded on the door. "Lana. Out. Now."

She yanked open the door, suitcase in hand and ran with him to the car.

He opened the passenger door and took the case from her.

Lana slid into the seat.

"Stay down," he warned and tossed the case into the back seat. Then he ran around the back of the car to the driver's side, slid behind the wheel and drove around the other side of the building, running through low hedges and emerging in another business's driveway.

"What are we going?" Lana asked.

"Getting the hell out of Dodge." The rental car spun out onto the street, and Trevor slammed his foot to the floor.

"I take it we were followed." Lana spun in her seat to stare out the back window. "I see headlights."

"Hang on." Trevor gritted his teeth. "I'm going to shake him."

Once again, Trevor wove through the streets, but everything he did, the man in the SUV seemed to anticipate.

Finally, Trevor pulled into an alley, parked the car behind a huge trash bin and shut off the engine and lights.

"I'd get out, but I don't think we have enough distance between us and our tail to risk opening the doors," Trevor said. "We don't want to have a light shine down, illuminating our position to our pursuer."

Lana unbuckled her seatbelt and sat on the edge

of the seat, her head swiveling back and forth. "I can't see much past the trash bin."

"I have a little bit of a view in the side mirror. If he's back there, I'll see him coming." He rested his hand on the ignition, ready to turn on the engine should they need to make another run for it.

"Anything?" Lana whispered.

"Nothing yet." Then a light appeared behind them, rolling past the narrow alley. "There he is."

Lana sat back in her seat, pulled her shoulder strap over her chest and buckled her seatbelt.

"Good girl," Trevor said.

"There you go again, talking to me like I'm a dog," she quipped, but her voice shook slightly.

"We'll be okay." He followed the light as the SUV passed their little alley and moved on. "He didn't turn this way."

"Shouldn't we take off and make a run for it in the opposite direction?" Lana asked.

"Not yet. He's smart. So far, he's anticipated a lot of my moves. Let's wait a few more minutes until he's farther away."

Lana nodded, sucked in a deep breath and let it out slowly.

A minute passed, then two. At the five-minute mark, Trevor fired up the engine and shifted into gear. Unfortunately, the car's safety settings wouldn't let him shift unless his foot was on the brake. The brake lights lit up, reflecting off the trash bin, illuminating the little alley.

"Time to go," Trevor said, and he pulled forward, heading out the other end of the alley. He eased off the accelerator, refusing to use the brakes unless he absolutely had to. He left his lights off and dimmed the dashboard.

Lana craned her neck, looking all around. When they emerged onto the street, she leaned far enough to look around him. "Looks like the coast is clear."

Trevor pulled onto the street and headed back the way they'd come. When he reached the next intersection, he was halfway through it when a dark vehicle, lights off, seemed to fly out of nowhere, coming at them from the left.

Slamming his foot to the pedal, Trevor shot the car forward. But not soon enough to avoid being hit. The other car smashed into the rear bumper of Trevor's rental car, sending them into a three-hundred-sixty-degree spin.

The car turned around and around before Trevor could get it to move another direction. When it finally slowed, he twisted the steering wheel, hit the curb, bumped up over the sidewalk and almost rammed into a building. At the last moment, the tires gripped the concrete, and he was able to swerve and miss the corner of a brick structure.

They bumped back onto the street and ran into the other vehicle where it faced away from them.

Trevor changed into low gear and pressed the accelerator, pushing the front bumper of his car into the driver's door of the other. Then he pushed the attacker's vehicle toward two heavy metal and concrete poles put in place to restrict vehicles from entering a narrow alley.

The driver struggled with the door on his vehicle, appeared to try to lower the window and finally aimed a handgun at the glass.

"Duck!" Trevor yelled and bent low.

A shot was fired. The bullet blasted through the windshield, making a perfectly round hole in the glass.

Shifting into reverse, Trevor backed away, spun the steering wheel and took off, leaving the attacker and his vehicle behind.

"Is he following?" Trevor barked.

"I think his car is hung up on the barriers," Lana said. "Looks like he's trying to climb out the other side."

"Stay down until we're well out of range of his weapon."

"You don't have to tell me twice." Lana ducked below the seat, peeking out every few seconds to see if the man had managed to get his vehicle going again.

"Call 911 and have the police pick him up." Trevor tossed her his cellphone.

Lana watched for street signs first, and then

placed the call giving directions to the man who'd attacked them. When the dispatcher asked for her name, she politely declined to give it and hung up. Holding the phone in her palm, she stared ahead at the road. "What now?"

"How about ditching this vehicle? We can catch a cab to your meeting with the FBI. No one will know what vehicle we'll arrive in until we get there."

Lana frowned. "Are you sure we won't put the driver in jeopardy?"

"All right." He blew out a harsh breath. "Then we find a quiet place to park until the FBI office opens." He glanced over at her. "How's watching the sunrise on the beach sound to you?"

"Wonderful," she said and leaned her head against the back of her seat. "As long as no one's shooting at us or trying to commit vehicular manslaughter, I'm good with that." She closed her eyes and yawned. "I'm not cut out for all this spy stuff."

"Why don't you sleep? I'll find a place that's safe."

"I'm going to take you up on that. I have a feeling this isn't over."

"I know it's not. If someone's this interested in shutting you up, he won't hesitate to try again."

Lana yawned again. "Wake me up when you want to catch some Zs. I'll try not to be too greedy about the amount of sleep I get."

He chuckled. "I'll be fine. Sleep, sweetheart."

For the next forty-five minutes, he drove through

the darkness, wishing he had a way to douse the automatic headlights. The car was a mess, and the bullet holes in the windshield caught the lights from oncoming vehicles, blinding him.

By the time he found a quiet stretch of beach where he could hide the car behind a rundown, abandoned shack, he was ready for some sleep, himself. But he didn't dare nod off. The way things had been going, the people after Lana would find them before Trevor could wake up enough to help.

No, he'd gone a few days without sleep with no ill effects before, other than being at less than his top mental ability. As soon as the FBI district office opened, he'd have Lana there, handing over all the information she'd gathered. Then she'd be out of the picture. He'd convince her to come to Montana with him to wait out the storm she'd unleash.

At least there, he'd see when the enemy was coming, and he'd have half a chance to pick him off before he got within range of Lana.

Trevor glanced over at Lana. Moonlight filtered through the shattered glass, giving him a view of her. Her head lolled to the side, and her eyelashes fanned across her cheeks in dark crescents.

She was every bit as beautiful now as she ever had been. Maybe more so. The year had aged her slightly, but she'd lost weight since Connolly's death, and she had dark shadows beneath her eyes. Her obsession with finding those responsible for her husband's death was both admirable and unnerving. She needed to move on with her life.

At the same time, Trevor was grateful for her perseverance. He hadn't known a bullet from behind had killed his friend. His hands clenched into fists. Connolly had been like a brother to him. He still couldn't believe the man was gone. All year, he'd fully expected that Connolly would knock on his door with his arms full of cases of beer, ready to settle back and watch a football game.

He'd had to remind himself daily that he couldn't just pick up a phone and call his friend. He could only imagine what Lana had gone through after the death of her spouse. She'd barely gotten on with living. She appeared to be obsessed with finding out who was responsible for Connolly's death and the underlying reasons for the attack.

Perhaps that was her way of handling the grief.

Trevor shrugged. Whatever helped her, he was all for it. But he was a little concerned about her fixation with the so-called evidence.

She should have handed it all over to law enforcement much sooner to avoid being caught in the crosshairs of some ruthless individuals.

Hell, they'd killed Connolly. Once blood was shed, people like that wouldn't hesitate to do it again to keep their secrets.

Trevor couldn't walk away from Lana now. She was in way over her head. Handing off to the FBI was the right thing to do, but Trevor feared it was a little late for Lana to extract herself from her predicament.

Passing the information to the FBI wouldn't necessarily stop what was happening. Nor would it erase the information from her files or her head.

Until the men at the root of the problem were caught, Lana would continue to be a target.

As soon as they had their meeting with the FBI, Trevor would whisk Lana as far away from California as he could get.

CHAPTER 6

L<small>ANA</small> W<small>OKE</small> to sunlight pushing through her slitted eyelids.

She blinked her eyes open, squinting in the brightness. She yawned and stretched. "What time is it?"

Trevor sat in the driver's seat, leaning back against the headrest, his eyes half-closed. "Almost seven o'clock," he murmured.

"My meeting is at nine o'clock. Shouldn't we be going? It might take a while to get there if the traffic is heavy." She yawned again and sat up straighter. "I'm ready to hand off this investigation and get back to living a semi-normal life."

"You and me both," Trevor said. He sat up and stared out at the beach in front him. "But it's such a beautiful morning. Want to go for a walk before we look for something to eat?"

Lana adjusted the seat to the upright position. "Sounds good. I need to move my legs after being stuck in a car all night. I'm sure you do, too." Before she got out of the vehicle, she glanced around. "Any sign of the guys who tried to kill us last night?"

Trevor shook his head. "I think your phone was the key. They were tracking you through it."

"How did they do that?" Lana pulled the visor down and studied her reflection in the mirror. What a mess. But it couldn't be helped. She was officially on the run.

"I don't know," Trevor said. "Maybe they slipped a tracking device into it. Or they hacked into your account and turned on a phone tracking app."

A shiver shook her body. "This past year has been a real eye-opener. Between men stealing money from the government, to the terrorists they were funding, to hackers on the dark web, I've been exposed to the seedier side of humankind. I don't think I can go back to living a normal life."

"The bad guys are a small percentage of the people here on earth. You can't judge everyone by their standard. There are plenty of good people out there who would help you sooner than hurt you."

Lana stared across at Trevor. "People like you?"

"I was thinking about my boss, Hank Patterson. He'd lay down his life for any one of the men working for him."

"Was he a Navy SEAL like you and Mason?" Lana asked.

Trevor grinned. "How'd you guess?"

"I had a hunch. Once a SEAL, always a SEAL, right? You have teamwork hammered into you from the moment you enter BUD/S training to the day you separate from the military."

"And beyond," Trevor added.

Lana nodded. "And beyond." As demonstrated by Trevor's commitment to his dead buddy to take care of his widow.

She hadn't made it easy for him to fulfill his promise. But then, she hadn't thought she was in mortal danger until yesterday.

"Are we going for that walk, or what?" She pushed open her door and stepped out. Stiff from being cramped in the car all night, she stood for a moment, moving each muscle to ease the discomfort. She could imagine Trevor, with his long body, had been even more uncomfortable sitting behind the steering wheel all night.

The Navy SEAL stood and stretched as if he were fresh from a good night's sleep.

She shook her head. The man probably hadn't slept for even fifteen minutes. "I don't know how you survive on so little sleep," she said.

"You learn to catch cat naps whenever you can."

She frowned, skeptical. "And will you find time to sleep today?"

He shrugged. "We'll see."

"I assume that means no." Again, she shook her head then held out her hand. "Come on, big guy. Let's take that walk. Then we have a meeting with the FBI."

He took her hand and strode with her to where the water lapped at the shore.

Lana kicked off her shoes and buried her toes in the cool, damp sand.

Trevor toed off his shoes as well and set them beside Lana's. Then he took her hand again, and they strolled at a leisurely pace along the shoreline in comfortable silence, like they had when she, Trevor and Mason had all been friends.

"Remember when you Mason, and I slept under the stars that night your team had the barbeque on the beach?"

Trevor nodded, his hand tightening on hers. "We'd all had too much to drink. We decided we had no business getting behind the wheel."

"That was a good night." She smiled, remembering how she'd gotten cold in the early morning. "You lent me your jacket."

He frowned. "Speaking of which, whatever happened to that jacket? I don't think you ever returned it."

She grinned up at him. "I didn't. I had it cleaned and was set to return it, but then you and Mason were deployed before I could get it back to you.

Somehow, it got pushed to the back of my closet, and I forgot about it." She squeezed his hand. "Remind me when we go back to my house to get it out."

"Keep it," he said, gruffly. "I have others."

"I thought it was nice of you to let me have it. I'm sure you were cold that morning as well, but you gave it to me, proving chivalry isn't dead." She leaned into his shoulder. It felt too darned good to be with him again. She sighed. "This past year, I missed you."

"Why didn't you tell me?" Trevor asked, his voice rough. "You know I would have been here had I known you needed me."

She shook her head. "I had to work through my grief in my own way. I guess it was selfish of me, especially when you and Mason were like brothers. I should have been there for you, too. But my head wasn't in a good place."

"I shouldn't have let you push me away."

"I didn't give you that choice."

He gave her a one-armed hug. "Well, I'm here now, and, this time, you're not getting rid of me so easily."

She smiled, her heart warming at his stubborn tone.

Trevor turned them around and guided her back to where they'd left their shoes.

"Have you thought about what you're going to do after this meeting with the FBI?" Trevor asked.

"I should probably go back to work at DHS," she

said, although her heart wasn't in the job anymore. She'd only taken it in order to dig into Mason's death. "One of my coworkers was helping me in my investigation. I'm betting he'll be worried when I don't show up for work today."

Trevor stiffened. "He? Is he more than a coworker to you?"

She chuckled. "No. He's just been helping me dig into department databases on the sly."

Trevor frowned. "You trust him?"

"I have no reason not to. He hasn't turned me in for meddling in department data. He was able to tap into the director's personal emails. That's where we found some clues that led us to a potential connection in Montana."

"You said the folks in Montana are survivalists planning on taking over the US government?"

"When I found their social media group, I thought, at first, that they were innocuous, but from what my contact on the dark web said, they have camps hidden in the mountains and backwoods of Montana, where they train like military commandos. Even my dark web guy said they're planning something. We discovered their funding can be traced back to the money that's supposed to be going to rebuild the Afghan infrastructure."

Trevor shoved a hand through his hair. "Are you sure your dark web guy isn't the one after you? You know a lot more than some people would want to get out."

She grimaced. "I haven't actually met my dark web guy. I met him online when I was searching for data on the primary contractors who are working the reconstruction projects in Afghanistan. He was also looking into their shenanigans."

"To blackmail them?"

She shrugged. "He may be dark web, but he's got it out for people who steal and misuse government money. Besides, I think he doesn't want to see his country implode."

"Are you sure he's a US citizen?"

"Pretty sure. Even though his online activities aren't exactly legal, he loves this country." She knew her answer sounded weak, but her gut told her WolfST6 was someone she could trust.

He shook his head. "It's so like you to trust strangers."

"I don't know what it is about my guy on the net, but he seems to care what happens to us."

"As long as he's not the one lobbing bullets your way, I'm okay with him." Trevor's jaw tightened. "But if he is the one, he's going down." He guided her back to the car then held the passenger door for her.

"Maybe we should call for a cab?" she said, eyeing the bullet holes and broken glass.

Trevor scrunched up his nose. "I think we can risk driving into town. But you may be right. We'll call too much attention to ourselves arriving in this thing. We'll park a few blocks from the FBI office and call a cab from there." He rounded the vehicle and slid behind the steering wheel.

"The FBI building is right off the interstate," Lana said. "There aren't any buildings around it to take cover in." She gave him a sheepish grin. "I've driven by it several times, tempted to go in and give them what little information I had. Up until now, I was too afraid they'd think I was some crazy person with a conspiracy theory."

"And now?" Trevor asked as he backed out of the bushes he'd parked behind and turned around on the highway.

Her lips thinned, images of the scene in her bedroom the night before flashing through her mind. She'd never been that scared in her life. "I'm convinced I must be onto something, if someone is scared enough to come after me."

Trevor nodded. "I'll feel a little better once we get to the FBI building."

"Me, too."

They traveled in silence until they reached the edge of the city. There, they drove through a fast-food establishment for coffee and breakfast sand-wiches. The clerk at the window raised his brows as their car pulled up. "Wow, and I thought I'd had a rough night." He gave them their order. "I hope your day gets better."

Lana chuckled as they left. "I bet we looked like gangsters to that kid."

"I'm not even sure how I'm going to explain the car to the rental company. Not that it matters. What matters is getting you safely out of San Diego after your meeting."

"Out of San Diego?" Lana's hand paused with her donut halfway to her mouth. "Who said I'm leaving San Diego?"

Trevor took a sip of coffee, and then set it in the cup holder. "Even after you turn over your data to the FBI, you still know too much. Whoever was after you last night won't give up just because you turned the case over to the Feds. They'll still be worried about what's in your head. What you can testify to."

She lowered her arm, the sugary donut no longer appealing to her. "You think I can't go home?"

He shook his head and shot a glance toward her. "Not until they catch the guys behind the attacks."

"But where will I go?" Lana hadn't considered being on the run for more than a day or two. "What if they don't catch them right away? I can't hide forever. Where will I go?"

Trevor cleared his throat. "You can come to Montana with me. We have a whole team of protectors who'll help me keep you safe."

"Mason's life insurance policy was good, but I can't afford to pay your entire team for any length of time."

"You don't have to pay for anything. I'm going to see to your protection. I promised Mason I'd look out for you. It's about time I did."

Lana glared. "I don't need a babysitter. I've made it this far on my own."

"And would you have made it through last night on you own?"

She clamped her mouth shut to keep from lying and saying she would have done just fine. The truth was, she wouldn't be alive if not for Trevor bursting through the window when he had. "No," she said finally. "But you can't earn a living if you're looking after me."

"I have some money put aside. Being a SEAL, we didn't get many opportunities to spend the money we made. I put it into investments. I have enough to live on for a couple years." He drove onto the interstate and picked up the speed.

The rental car, received curious stares from passing motorists. The vehicle had been crashed into several times and had been riddled with bullet holes throughout the body and windshield. It also made funny noises, but the engine still worked, and the tires were intact. Lana was thankful for that. The closer they could get to the FBI building, the better off they'd be.

"Montana," Lana muttered. "I've never been to Montana."

"It's a beautiful state. I think you'll like it there."

A thought occurred to her. "How close is Eagle Rock to the Bitterroot Mountains?"

"About a three-hour drive." Trevor frowned. "Why?"

"If we could find the people who are plotting the overthrow of the US government, we might also find the evidence the FBI will need to shut them down."

Trevor's foot left the accelerator. "Lana. You aren't going after the terrorists." The vehicle slowed. Other cars went around them, their drivers honking at them. "Get this straight...You will *not*...I repeat...*not* go after terrorists. Do you understand?"

"You can't tell me what I can and cannot do," she said, though her voice lacked the strength it should have had.

Anger wasn't what she was seeing in Trevor's eyes. She saw worry and concern. "Okay, I won't go after the terrorists. But we will be close, won't we?"

"Yes. And no, we aren't going after them." Trevor resumed the posted speed with a white-knuckled grip on the steering wheel. "I get the feeling you have a death wish."

"Not unless it's a death wish for the people responsible for Mason's murder." She sat with her uneaten donut in her hand, her jaw tight and her pulse pounding through her veins. "The contractors, the terrorists and the shooters need to be brought to justice."

"But *you* aren't the one to do it."

Her blood boiled up, her temper with it. "If I don't do something, who will? The military is willing to let Mason's death go as a KIA. They're willing to close the books and sweep the rest under the rug."

"You should have contacted me as soon as you learned what you did about Mason's death. I would have helped and kept you from becoming a target."

"If I'd brought you in early on, I wouldn't have my dark web contact. I wouldn't have gone to work for the DHS, and I wouldn't have gotten help with my research through my coworker. I'd have little more than I started out with."

"You don't know that."

She sighed and dropped the donut into the paper bag it came in. "That's all in the past. We can't dwell on it. We have to think about what comes next."

Though she was irrationally angry with Trevor, Lana knew he was right. She couldn't go back to her home. Not when someone was gunning for her. Handing over her information to the FBI might not get her off the hook. She had to go into hiding until the FBI had a chance to follow her leads.

Gritting her teeth for what was to come, she took a deep breath and said, "Montana, it is."

CHAPTER 7

TREVOR PARKED the damaged vehicle two miles from the FBI building. He tucked it between two older buildings with peeling paint and a pile of weathered wooden pallets. No one would see the vehicle from the street, and they were within easy walking distance of a gas station where they could use a phone to call a cab.

"I think we'll have to leave your suitcase in the rental car."

Lana nodded. "I'm sure the FBI would have an issue if I brought a suitcase into their office."

Trevor nodded. "They might think you were bringing a bomb."

"Can't be too careful these days. Especially in government buildings," Lana noted.

They walked together to the nearby gas station. When Trevor asked to use a telephone, the attendant behind the counter gave them a narrow-eyed look. "Don't you have a cell phone?"

"If we did, we'd use it." Trevor gave the attendant a smile to soften his retort. "I dropped it in the ocean," Trevor lied.

The guy's face relaxed. "I've done that." He handed the phone and a phone book over the counter to Trevor. "Help yourself."

Lana perused the convenience store for anything that might help them disguise themselves. She found two LA Dodgers baseball caps and a couple of light-weight rain jackets. It wasn't much, but it might help them get into the cab and into the FBI building without becoming targets again.

Trevor ordered the cab, paid for the items and a couple bottles of water. They dressed in the rain jackets and caps and waited inside the building. Trevor's gaze searched the parking lot, the surrounding streets and every passing vehicle. He couldn't leave it up to luck to get Lana to the FBI building safely. He had to be on his toes, and aware at all times. Fatigue threatened to dull his senses, so he downed a high-energy drink. By the time the cab finally arrived, his heart was pumping, and he was wide awake and jittery. Not a place he liked to be, but he couldn't do anything about it now.

The cab pulled into the gas station. After a quick check around the area, Trevor escorted Lana out of the convenience store. He assisted Lana into the back seat and slid in next to her.

Lana gave the driver the address and sat back, a frown denting her forehead.

Trevor reached for her hand held it for the next twenty minutes, hoping to reassure her.

She sat stiffly beside him, one hand resting over her big purse containing her notes and laptop. "What if they don't listen? What if they do nothing?"

"You have to let them know what you found." Trevor lowered his voice to a whisper. "If there is a terrorist plot underway, it's your duty to inform them. Your information could stop a deadly attack and save many lives."

"When you put it that way, I have an obligation to turn over the information. Sitting on it could cost lives."

"Exactly." The morning traffic had stalled on the interstate highway. Instead of a road, it appeared to be a parking lot.

Lana fidgeted beside him, craning her neck to see beyond the car in front of their cab. "What's taking so long?" She glanced at her watch. "We're going to be late."

"I'm sure they won't turn you away," Trevor said. He understood how Lana felt. He was ready to get the meeting over with and hit the road to Montana. He'd have to figure out a way to get there without alerting Lana's attackers to their mode of transportation or destination.

As soon as they left the cab, he'd call the pilot who'd flown him to San Diego and see if he was still in town.

The traffic finally moved, and the taxi crept along the interstate for the next mile to the exit. At the front entrance of the FBI building, the cab driver pulled up and jumped out to open the door for Trevor and Lana. Trevor got out, scanned the area for potential threats, and then helped Lana out of the backseat.

With his arm wrapped protectively around her, he walked with her into the building.

Once inside, they went through a metal detector and approached the reception desk.

Lana pulled her driver's license from her wallet and handed it to the clerk. "I'm here to meet with Special Agent James Thompson."

The woman scanned her license and held out her hand for Trevor's. He handed his to the woman and waited while she made visitors passes for them. "Have a seat, while I let Agent Thompson know you've arrived."

Trevor and Lana walked over to the seating area. Lana sank onto the edge of one of the leather chairs.

"Do you think it would be a bad idea for me to call in to work?" Lana asked. "I feel bad that I'm not there when I'm scheduled to work today."

"It should be okay."

"On your cell phone?" she asked.

"I don't see why not. We should be safe inside this building, and whoever was after you last night, probably already knows you're here today." He handed her his cell phone. "But don't tell them where you're going."

"I won't." Lana entered her work number and waited for someone on the other end to answer.

"Oh, hello, Peter. I thought this was Margaret's number." She paused. "Oh, I forgot she was out of the office until next week. I'm sorry, but something came up last night. I won't be in the office the rest of this week." She shook her head. "No, no. I'm okay, but I had an...emergency come up, and I have to take care of it. I'm sorry for the short notice." She stared up at Trevor. "No, it's nothing to do with our special project. If you could let Mr. Powell know I won't be in, I'd really appreciate it. You can tell him I'm sick or something. Thanks." She ended the call and handed the phone back to Trevor. "I felt like I should have warned Peter about what happened. He's been so helpful with my research." A frown wrinkled her brow. "You don't think he'll be in danger, do you?"

"Did he know you were going to take the information to the FBI?"

She shook her head. "I made that decision on my own. I didn't want to implicate him in any way, in case we got in trouble for hacking into the DHS databases."

"He should be okay. You did right by leaving your emergency vague."

She inhaled and let go of a long, slow breath. Then she hugged herself around the middle. "I don't feel good about any of this."

"Just hand it off to the FBI, and we'll get you somewhere safe until all this blows over."

She nodded. "Okay. At least I know I can trust you."

"What about Peter?"

"He's all right. He doesn't like it when people steal from the government any more than I do. And he understands how important it is for me to get to the truth about Mason's death."

It hurt Trevor to know Lana was still grieving over her dead husband. Why else would she be a year out from his death and still pushing to get answers? "Hopefully, the FBI will get to the bottom of what's going on. But for now, you need to get away from San Diego."

She nodded. "I know you're right, but I feel like I'm abandoning my work...and Mason," she added softly.

A twinge of pain settled in his chest. "You're not abandoning either. You're taking the next step and turning it over to the professionals. They have more resources and an entire organization they can tap into to get the answers you've been digging for."

She smiled up at him. "You're right, as usual. I've put my faith in you. Now I just need to let the system work."

Trevor didn't like the way her shoulders drooped, or the fact her mouth turned downward in a frown, but there was nothing he could do at that point to cheer her. They had to get the investigation into the hands of the FBI.

With too much energy to sit, Trevor paced the floor. He called the pilot who'd flown him down from Montana and was just lucky enough to catch him before he headed back to Big Sky country. The pilot promised to wait for him and Lana.

With the method of transport to Montana in place, Trevor had nothing left to do but walk from one end of the waiting area to the other. He focused his attention on the elevator doors behind the reception desk.

The elevator was a busy place. It opened and closed on people going up and those coming down to leave the building.

A man with salt-and-pepper hair exited the elevator and walked directly toward Lana. "Mrs. Connolly, nice to meet you." He held out his hand.

Lana placed hers in his. "Thank you for taking the time to see me."

"I'm interested to hear what you have to say." He

waved toward a door on the far side of the lobby. "Please, join me in the conference room."

Lana motioned toward Trevor. "I brought my... friend with me. I'd like him to sit in on this conversation."

Agent Thompson held out his hand. "James Thompson."

"Trevor Anderson." Trevor gave the man's hand a firm shake.

Thompson's eyes narrowed slightly. "Prior military?"

Trevor nodded. "Navy."

"Thank you for your service," Thompson said. "Spent four years in the Marine Corps myself. Deployed to the sandbox twice before I suffered an injury that sidelined my military career and gave me all this gray hair."

"I'm surprised you got on with the FBI. Don't they have strict physical standards?"

Thompson nodded. "They do. But I recovered enough to pass their fitness tests. And here I am." He waved toward the door. "Please, join me in the conference room. I want to hear what Mrs. Connolly has to say."

Thirty minutes later, Lana had given Agent Thompson all the information she'd acquired, leaving out how she'd acquired some of it from a deep web hacker.

Agent Thompson sat back in his chair. "This is all

interesting. I'll run it by other agents in the department and see if anyone is working a similar scenario. If not, I'll take on the task of following your leads. Thank you for all the work you've done so far."

"I don't want your thanks," Lana said. "I need to know someone will work this case."

Trevor leaned forward. "She's not safe, as it is. I doubt seriously she'll be safe until you find the people who attacked her last night."

"I'll reach out to the San Diego Police Department detective in charge of the investigation into the shooting at Mrs. Connolly's home." Thompson gave Trevor and Lana a chin lift. "In the meantime, how can I get hold of you two?"

Trevor glanced at Lana. "You won't be able to get in touch with us. I'm taking Lana away from San Diego. We'll be in touch with you periodically. I don't want whoever tried to kill Lana to follow us."

Thompson nodded. "I understand. But we might have questions for you, Mrs. Connolly."

"We'll be in touch often enough to answer any of your queries," Lana said, challenging Trevor with a raised eyebrow. "I want the people responsible for my husband's death to be brought to justice, preferably before they can execute any plan to overthrow the government."

"Believe me when I say, we take these threats seriously," Thompson said.

Lana nodded. "Good. I didn't spend a year of my life chasing wild geese. These threats are real."

She handed him a thumb drive. "This drive contains all the information I've gathered for the past year. It includes the names of people in high positions within their organizations, locations of terrorist cells hiding in the mountains of Montana and some government officials responsible for the safety of our nation, who are involved with the plot to overthrow our government. Guard it carefully. Someone didn't want me to live to pass it on." Lana pushed to her feet. "I'll call for an update in a couple days."

Thompson took the flash drive. "Thank you for all you did to amass this data. I'll be sure to move on it, once I check it out."

"Don't sit on it," Lana cautioned. "I might have already taken too long to bring it to your attention. If they truly are planning an attempt to overthrow the government, they've had over a year to prepare."

"On it, Mrs. Connolly. And when we get to the bottom of it, we'll do our best to let you know what happened." He stood and held out his hand. "It's citizens like you who help us more than you can imagine."

Lana's cheeks blossomed with color. "I don't know about that, but I do know someone is worried about this information getting out. Now that it is, they might move faster."

"Understood. Please be safe, wherever you go," Thompson said.

"I have every intention of keeping her safe," Trevor said. "You can count on that."

"Is there anything we can do for you?" Thompson asked.

Trevor gave him a crooked smile. "As a matter of fact, there is. We could use a ride to the local general aviation airport. We had to ditch the rental car after it was targeted several times."

"I'll get one of my guys to give you a lift. And I'll work with the local police about the attack on your vehicle and have someone retrieve the rental car and deal with the rental agency."

"Thank you," Lana said.

"Yes. Thank you." Trevor shook hands with the agent, his mind already a thousand miles ahead of where they were standing.

Thompson left them in the lobby, promising to send someone down to take them to the airport.

"What do you think?" Trevor asked Lana.

"I liked Agent Thompson. I think he really cares."

"Does it help set your mind at ease about the investigation?" Trevor watched the play of emotions rushing across Lana's face.

Lana tilted her head, her eyes narrowing. "Yes and no."

"What do you mean?"

"I'm worried I haven't done enough. That the FBI

will have to dig a lot deeper. They don't have my connection to the dark web. They might not get the same information to back my assumptions. The people involved may already have caught wind that the FBI will be looking into their business. They could be packing up as we speak and bugging out to some other state to set up shop again."

"You have a point," Trevor agreed. "We don't know if the bad guys in this situation have already packed up and moved out ahead of a shit-storm of Feds investigating them. But back to the idea that you haven't done enough. You've done well beyond enough. You don't have to do anything else but hide until they figure this thing out and arrest those who've been trying to kill you."

A young man exited the elevator and approached them. "Mr. and Mrs. Connolly?"

Trevor's heart skipped several beats at being addressed as Mr. Connolly.

Lana answered, "That's us."

"I'm Randy Gaither. If you're ready, I'll take you to the airport now," the young man said.

"Thank you," Lana said. She hooked her hand through Trevor's elbow and followed the young man out of the building.

Trevor didn't let down his guard for a moment. The hairs on the back of his neck stood at attention as they climbed into the backseat of the man's car.

Oh, he trusted the young man, but he had a feeling they were being watched.

Giving Randy the address of the small, general aviation airport, Trevor leaned over the back of the driver's seat and said, "I want you to pretend we're being followed and do your best to shake anyone off your tail. Got that?"

The driver frowned. "Excuse me?"

Trevor repeated his instructions. "Have you been trained on driving techniques used to avoid being followed?"

The man shook his head, staring into Trevor's eyes in the rearview mirror. "I'm just the mail clerk. I have to drive by the airport to get to the local UPS office and collect a package that didn't make it on the morning run."

"Humor me, will ya?" Trevor leaned over the back of the front seat. "The young lady in your car has had a very frustrating night. I'd like to know she'll make it to the airport without being run off the road or shot at again."

Randy's brows rose. "You were run off the road? Shot at? When?"

Lana gave the young man a small smile. "Yes, we were attacked, but obviously we made it out of the situation just fine. "

"We made it by zigzagging through neighborhoods and losing our tail," Trevor emphasized. "Just to be conservative, would you take us the long way to the airport, ducking into neighborhoods to keep our vehicle on the downlow."

"I can do that," the young man said, sitting straighter.

"Good," Trevor said. "Then do it."

Randy eased out of the parking lot and onto the access road. Soon they were on the interstate headed toward the airport.

Lana and Trevor sat sideways in their seats alternating between looking forward and backward. With as many vehicles on the road as there were, they'd find it difficult to spot one following them. Once they exited the interstate, Randy took a circuitous route to avoid being spotted by someone bent on attacking them.

The smaller roads meant fewer vehicles to keep track of.

"Do you think anyone is following us?" Lana asked.

"I can't say for certain, but I haven't seen any particular car following for more than a block or two behind us."

"This is fun," Randy said. "I've applied to become an agent. If I make it in, do you think we'll do things like this?"

Lana chuckled. "You'll have to ask Agent Thompson. I'm not familiar with what all the agents do."

They arrived at the hanger the pilot had indicated and thanked Randy for bringing them.

Trevor slipped an arm around Lana and hustled her into the hanger. They weren't out of danger yet. The plane had to be a mile in the sky before Trevor would feel like they were out of range of a shooter's sights.

The woman at the desk informed them the pilot was performing pre-flight checks on the aircraft. They were to join him on the tarmac. "The restrooms are down that hall."

"You'll want to make use of their amenities," Trevor suggested. "This is a small aircraft. No facilities on board."

Lana shook her head. "I'm good."

The receptionist hit the button to open the sliding glass doors.

Trevor and Lana walked out into the San Diego sunshine.

Several airplanes lined the tarmac.

Lana shaded her eyes. "Which plane is it?"

Trevor pointed to a white plane with gold and black trim. "That one."

The pilot emerged from behind the tail and waved.

Moments later, they had boarded the four-seater, single engine aircraft.

Lana chose to sit in the back seat, allowing Trevor to ride in the seat next to the pilot.

As they left the ground, Trevor held his breath. They were at their most vulnerable until they achieved enough altitude to get them out of a gunman's range.

As the aircraft climbed higher into the sky, Trevor relaxed and turned to glance back at Lana.

She sat with her fingers digging into the armrests, her eyes rounded.

"Are you all right?"

She nodded. "Just fine. Have I told you I've never flown in anything smaller than a one-hundred-passenger plane?"

He smiled. "Quintin's a good pilot. He'll get us there safely. Why don't you go to sleep? We'll stop once on the way up to refuel. Other than that, it should be an uneventful flight."

"You know that for certain?" she quipped.

Quintin chuckled. "I'll do my best to keep the plane in the air when it's supposed to be. Sorry we don't have a flight attendant, but we can't afford the extra weight on board."

"Don't worry about me," Lana said. "Just concentrate on flying the damned plane."

"Yes, ma'am."

Both Trevor and Quintin chuckled.

The glare on Lana's face only made Trevor smile more. He reached back and touched her hand. "We're going to be all right. And I think you'll like Montana."

"Ask me when I get there. Right now, I'm just going to sit here and will this puddle-jumper to remain in the air. I'd hate to think I'd lived through a gunman shooting at me only to die in an airplane crash."

"You're not going to die in an airplane crash," Trevor assured her. "Close your eyes and pretend you're drifting among the clouds. In effect, you are."

She did as he told her and closed her eyes.

Trevor smiled at the wrinkle creasing her brow. He wanted to crawl into the back seat, pull her into his arms and kiss away her worry. The woman had experienced enough trauma in the past twenty-four hours. Flying in a small aircraft shouldn't have caused her so much anxiety. But it did.

Still, she didn't come apart. Instead, she sat in her seat with her eyes closed until her breathing grew deeper and her face relaxed. She'd fallen asleep.

Trevor wished all her worries could be swept away. They couldn't. But that was why he was bringing her to Montana. At least there, he could take care of her, protect her and finally fulfill his promise to his old friend.

And maybe beneath the big sky full of stars, she can fall in love with me.

As soon as the thought popped into Trevor's head, he chastised himself for even thinking it. He wouldn't poach on Mason's girl. It wasn't right, even if his friend was dead. Especially since his friend was dead.

Trevor sighed and faced the windshield, the bright blue sky and the puffs of clouds. Looking out at the heavens, he found it hard to believe there were such bad people in the world that they'd hurt a defenseless woman.

But then, Trevor had witnessed some of the worst sides of humanity. He just hoped he could keep people like that way from Lana.

CHAPTER 8

LANA MUST HAVE FALLEN ASLEEP. When she opened her eyes again, the plane had grown silent and still. She jerked upright, her eyes wide and her heart racing. What had happened? Were they still in the sky? On the ground? Dead?

A fuel truck rumbled by and stopped in front of the airplane. A man climbed down, grounded the aircraft and stuck a nozzle into the fuel tank of the right wing.

"Trevor?" she asked softly into her headset.

"I'm right here," he responded. But not into her headset.

He stood outside the door of the aircraft on the ground. "You were sleeping too well. I didn't want to wake you. But now that you are, do you want to use the facilities while we're here? We won't stop again until we reach Bozeman, Montana."

Lana climbed out of the airplane. Still sleepy, she stumbled.

Trevor caught her and held her against his body until she had her feet firmly on the ground.

Still, Lana didn't want to move away. The air was cool, and his body was warm. And he smelled good.

She inhaled and let out the breath slowly. God, she'd missed being held in someone's arms. Someone she loved and who loved her in return. She'd been happy with Mason. They had started a good life together. Had he lived, she might have been pregnant by now.

But now, she stood in Trevor's arms, wishing she could start a new life with him. How could she be so disloyal to Mason's memory? Or was it being disloyal? They had all been such close friends. Wouldn't Mason want her to be happy—to fall in love again? He'd want her to have the children they'd always planned. Lana knew this deep in her heart. But would Trevor see it that way? She doubted it.

She sighed and pushed to arm's length. "Which way do I go?"

He pointed, and she walked away. No use dreaming about something that would never happen.

In the meantime, she would do as he asked and make sure she didn't make his life any more difficult than she already had.

A few minutes later, they were all back in the

airplane. This time Trevor climbed into the back seat with Lana and put on his flight headset.

Lana settled her headset over her ears and adjusted the mic. "Why aren't you up front?"

"I wanted to see the view from back here," he said. "And maybe catch one of those cat naps I told you about." He smiled. "Unless I'm crowding you. Maybe you'd like to sit up front with Quintin...?"

"No," she answered too fast. "I'm good with sitting in the back. Quintin seems to know what he's doing, and I don't want to bump anything that will throw him off."

Quintin chuckled. "I've got the controls. You two relax and enjoy the ride."

Lana snorted and muttered beneath her breath, "Easy for him to say."

"I heard that," Quintin said.

"Sorry," Lana said. "Nothing against your flying, but these little planes take some getting used to."

Again, Quintin laughed. "Understood, and no offense taken."

When the little plane left the ground, Lana dug her fingernails into Trevor's arm, glad he was beside her as they took that terrifying leap into the sky.

"Taking off is the easy part. Landing is what makes me shaky," Trevor admitted.

"What? You don't like my landings?"

"Seeing the runway coming up at you so fast was

a bit unsettling the first few times I sat in the copilot's seat," Trevor said.

"You tell me this now that we're in the air?" Lana said.

"You slept through the last landing and lived to tell about it. Oh, wait. You can't tell anyone about it, because you were sound asleep." Trevor squeezed her hand and leaned into her shoulder. "You'll be fine. Quintin set this baby down so lightly, you slept right through it."

The next couple of hours Lana drifted in and out of sleep. Beside her, Trevor slept soundly. He had to be exhausted, having stayed up the night before.

Lana took the opportunity to study his face while he wasn't watching. She memorized everything from his five-o'clock shadow to the slight dimple in his chin. She'd always loved how deep and dark his brown eyes were. At first, she'd thought they were black, until she'd seen the gold flecks. He'd let his hair grow a little longer than the high-and-tight cut he'd worn in San Diego at Mason's funeral. A lock of his dark brown hair fell over his forehead.

It was all Lana could do to keep from reaching out to smooth his hair back. He'd aged some in the past year; the lines around his eyes were deeper. And he'd gotten more sun; his skin was darker. He looked healthy, but was he happy? She still didn't know if he had a girlfriend back home in Montana. He'd grown up in that state. He might have a high school sweetheart he'd reconnected with.

A dull ache spread through her chest at the thought of Trevor loving another woman. Was that how he'd felt when she'd chosen to marry Mason?

Hell, he'd never asked her to marry him and probably never would have. Lana wanted children. Mason had offered her a life with children in it. Now, she had neither the children nor Mason.

Her eyes stung. She blinked back the tears. A lump lodged in her throat, and she swallowed hard to ease it.

The roar of the engine lulled her into sleep again. When she woke and looked out the window, they were coming in for a landing. Her body tensed, and she gripped the armrest. From what she could see, the ground seemed to be rushing up at them at an alarming rate. She'd never noticed this phenomenon in one of the big jet airliners. Why hadn't she noticed it until now?

Trevor's big hand captured hers and held tight.

She leaned into him, tempted to tell him that she loved him. If they didn't live, she'd die knowing she'd at least tried to tell him how she felt.

But the wheels of the landing gear touched the ground before she could open her mouth. And then they were taxiing to a stop outside a small terminal.

"Welcome to Montana," Quintin said.

When the prop stopped spinning, Quintin opened the door and climbed out.

Trevor went next, and then Lana.

Trevor gripped her around the waist and eased her to the ground. "All right?"

She nodded, breathless and very much off kilter. Her dreams had been filled with a naked Trevor wearing nothing but that darned towel.

"You don't look all right." He touched a hand to her forehead. "You're flushed. Are you running a fever?"

Her cheeks burned even more. But she couldn't tell him that his touch made her flustered, and his body so close made her breath all wonky. And if she didn't get away from him soon, she'd lean up on her toes and kiss him.

"Anderson, glad you made it back safely," a voice called out.

Trevor turned, giving Lana the space she needed to pull herself together.

When she looked around, she noted a tall man wearing jeans and a cowboy hat.

He smiled and engulfed Trevor in a bone-crunching hug and gave him several hearty claps on his back. "Glad you made it back so quickly." He let go of Trevor and faced Lana. "I see you've brought company."

"Hank Patterson, meet Lana Connolly."

"Ms. Connolly, pleased to meet you." When Lana

held out a hand, Hank bypassed it to pull her into as big a hug as he'd given Trevor, less the heavy-handed pats on the back. "Connolly..." Hank stood back, his eyes narrowing. "Connolly. Con Man Connolly." His eyes widened. "Are you Con Man's wife?"

"Widow," Lana corrected. "Mason was killed in action last year."

Hank nodded, his smile fading. "I heard about that." He shot a glance toward Trevor. "Connolly was a good guy. I'm sorry for your loss and ours."

"Thank you," Lana said. "Are you the Hank Trevor talked about? The man who set up the Brotherhood Protectors?"

Hank's grin was back. "You can blame me."

"I understand you're doing a lot of good with your organization. I looked it up when Trevor told me he was going to work for you."

"I only hire the best. Men who are dedicated to providing only the best protection to the people who hire us." He clapped his hand together. "You two must be hungry. Sadie is at the house, cooking up a storm. She'd skin me alive if I didn't bring you home for dinner." He held out his hand to the pilot. "You too, Quintin. That's a lot of flying in such a short time."

"Give Sadie a hug for me and tell her I'll take a rain check. My family would like to see me as well, and I promised to take my son fishing tomorrow."

"Will do," Hank said. "Say hello to your mother

for me. Tell her Sadie tried that recipe for homemade peach cobbler and it was so good, I ate the entire pan in two days." He patted his flat belly. "Had to work out three times a day to keep it from sticking."

Quintin grinned. "I'll tell her. She's been so busy looking after the kids, she barely has time to cook more than the basics anymore."

"When are you going to hire a nanny?"

"I've been thinking about it. Mom and Dad are getting the itch to hit the road again in their motorhome. I just can't imagine finding someone who can deal with Michael. He's a handful. Always into something. Even Mom pulls her hair out trying to keep up with him when I'm away."

"I'll ask Sadie to put out some feelers. She's good at finding people."

"I'd appreciate any leads you might have. I'm out of ideas, and I'm getting more work than I can handle. Word of mouth spread fast about my flying service."

Hank grinned. "Again, that Sadie is good at finding people. She put the word out among her acting friends, and they can't get to Montana fast enough."

"Tell her thanks. I promised her I'd bring the kids by for a play date with Emma soon. I'll be sure to make that happen."

Lana listened to the exchange, amazed at the familiarity and companionship these men displayed.

She hadn't realized how much she missed being a part of Mason and Trevor's team gatherings until that moment. A strong yearning washed over her. She'd liked being one of the group, hanging out with Mason's friends and their families.

With Mason gone, she'd lost, not only her husband, but the extended SEAL team family. Though that had been her fault. The men had tried to include her, but she hadn't felt like being a "hanger on." Again, she swallowed hard to dislodge the lump forming in her throat.

Hank said goodbye to Quintin and waved a hand toward a big, black, king-cab truck. "Lana, Anderson, your chariot awaits."

Trevor held the front passenger seat door open for Lana. She passed it by and opened the rear door. "You and Hank probably have some catching up to do," she said by way of explaining.

"You sure?" He helped her into the backseat and secured the seat belt across her lap, his fingers brushing her hip as he snapped the buckle in place.

A surge of heat ripped through her body from the point he touched to her center. She couldn't get over how much she wanted this man. Being celibate for a year was wreaking havoc on her libido. She just didn't know how she'd feel making love to Trevor. The last man she'd had sex with had been Mason. Would it be weird to make love with her husband's best friend?

Probably. She shouldn't even consider it.

Then why did she light up like a Roman candle every time he brushed against her?

Pushing thoughts of sex out of her mind, she sat with her hands folded in her lap, willing her core to cool.

As soon as they'd touched down in Bozeman, Montana, Trevor had sensed a lifting of his spirits, a sense of coming home. Something felt right about having Lana on his stomping grounds, away from the threats against her life. Away from where she and Mason had made a life together.

Trevor had no lingering memories of Mason or Lana in Montana like he had in San Diego. Everywhere he'd turned in the southern California city, he'd remembered something they'd done as a trio. The bar they'd frequented, their favorite restaurant. The beach they'd partied on with the team. Images of Mason and Lana getting married, Mason and Lana laughing at something one of the guys said. He couldn't get away from them in San Diego.

Montana, on the other hand, was a clean slate. A place he could start over with Lana. Here, she was just Lana. A girl he cared about. Not the wife of his best friend. At least he could pretend more easily here than he could back in California.

She was still Mason's widow, but she, too, had the opportunity to start over here. If she wanted to.

Trevor would never want Lana to forget Mason. Hell, Mason had been as much a brother to Trevor as he had been a husband to Lana. He'd never forget the man who'd meant so much to him.

The gap he'd left in Trevor's life remained a gaping maw. Someday, Trevor hoped he would get over the anger, sadness and guilt he'd harbored since the day Mason had died.

Trevor had second-guessed himself at least a hundred times over the past year. He should have taken point, instead of Mason. Point man always had the most danger to face. Newly married, Mason had no business being point man.

Trevor had no one waiting for him to come home. He'd have been a better sacrifice to the mission. Mason had deserved to live a long, happy life with Lana.

He'd lain awake nights wondering if he'd wished his friend dead so that he could have Lana.

That's why, when she'd pushed him away, he'd gone willingly. If he'd stayed, he would never have forgiven himself for making a play for Mason's widow.

Now, she was in Montana, and a year had passed since Mason's death.

A ripple of excitement lit his veins and sent blood and adrenaline shooting through his entire body. She was here, and he didn't have to pretend he didn't want her.

Trevor drew in a deep breath and willed his pulse to slow. Now wasn't the time to come on to Lana. She was in danger. Someone had tried more than once to kill her. Until the threat had been neutralized, Trevor couldn't move on his feelings. He wouldn't know if any emotion she returned would come from gratitude or true love.

He knew she had feelings for him. Could they be more than that of a sister for her brother? Could they move past best friends to become lovers?

"Tell me what's been going on since you lit out of here yesterday like your tail was on fire." Hank shifted into drive and pulled away from the airport and onto the highway that led to Eagle Rock.

For the next thirty minutes, Trevor and Lana filled Hank in on what was happening in Lana's world.

When they finished, Hank let out a long, low whistle. "Lana, you seem to have touched a nerve."

"Yes, sir. It appears so," she said.

"I'll be sure to put the other members of the Brotherhood on alert should you experience anymore attacks." He gave a slight chin lift to Trevor. "Say the word, and we'll pull some of the others in to provide additional protection."

"Thank you," Trevor said. "I'm pretty sure we

made it out of San Diego without leaving much of a trail."

"I wouldn't rest on my laurels at this juncture."

"Believe me, I'm not." Trevor cast a glance over his shoulder at Lana. "I won't let anything happen to her."

Lana gave him a quick smile. "I appreciate all you and your team are doing for me," she said. "But I hate to tie up too many people, babysitting me. I'm sure you have more important things to do."

"You're important. And we won't forget that," Hank said. "Besides, Sadie loves when there are more females moving into the Eagle Rock area. She likes having hen parties with the ladies."

"Hen parties?" Lana chuckled. "Did you really just say hen parties?"

"That's what my mother would have called them. You know when women get together, exchange recipes, quilt, have play dates with their children. That kind of thing."

"Only women?" Lana snorted. "Sounds kind of sexist to me."

"Oh, it's not always all women. Chuck Johnson comes and brings his three-year-old niece, Lyla, and Boomer's baby girl Maya. All the children think he's the best. He gets down on the floor and plays with them. And he's good at cooking, and he also knows how to sew. Yeah, he's a great addition to the hen parties." Hank twisted his lips. "Hmmm. Guess I better come up with a better name for those get togethers. Chuck would string me up by my toes for calling him a hen."

"Well, since I don't sew or cook, and I don't have children, will Sadie write me off?"

"No way," Trevor said. "She can talk to anyone. The woman is gifted on the social scene. She finds something good and interesting in everyone and makes them feel at home the minute they meet."

Hank laughed. "That's Sadie. I guess that's why she's so wildly popular with movie goers. She can work with any director and doesn't go diva on anyone. Her heart is pure gold, and I love her more than she can ever know."

Lana's chest tightened. Hearing a man admit to how much he loved his wife made her wish she had such a relationship. She stared at the back of Trevor's head. Would she ever find that kind of love?

Hank left the highway and stopped at a gate with the words White Oak Ranch written on a sign that arched over the road. He pressed a button on a remote control, and the wrought-iron gate swung open.

"Smile and wave at the security camera. I'm betting Sadie's been watching, waiting for us to get here." Hank waved at the camera attached to the corner of the sign and drove through. He paused long enough to make certain the gate closed behind them, before resuming the drive up to the main house.

When Hank pulled up in front of a sprawling cedar and rock ranch house, a beautiful woman stepped out on the porch. Her blond hair and blue eyes were just as impressive in person as they were on the big screen.

Lana couldn't believe she was about to meet the screen legend, Sadie McClain, Hank Patterson's wife.

Trevor helped her down from the truck, took her hand and walked with her to the steps leading up to the wide, covered porch.

Sadie smiled as she balanced a pretty, blond-haired, blue-eyed baby on her hip. "You must be Lana." She gave Lana a hug. The baby took the opportunity to grab a handful of Lana's hair and hold on.

When Sadie leaned back, the baby kept hold of the hair, pulling Lana with her.

"Emma, darling, you can't have Lana's hair. Let go." Sadie worked at opening the baby's fist, so Lana could free her hair.

Lana laughed and stepped back. "Not only is she adorable, she knows what she wants and goes after it." Lana held out her hands. "May I hold her?"

Sadie's pretty brow twisted., "Are you sure you want to risk getting your hair pulled again?"

"She's not going to hurt me."

"Don't be so sure," Sadie warned. "I still have a bruise beneath my chin where she headbutted me."

"I'll take my chances."

Sadie sighed. "Don't say I didn't warn you." And she handed Emma to Lana.

Emma stared at Lana, her brow forming a V over the bridge of her nose.

Lana held her breath and cringed, waiting for Emma to erupt into an ear-splitting scream.

When the child didn't go ape-shit crazy, Lana let go of the breath she'd held and smiled at Emma. "Hey, little girl. Who's holding you now?"

The baby stared at her and waved her hand. That little hand made contact with Lana's ear and held on.

Lana laughed.

Sadie reached for Emma's hand. "Here, let me get her to let go."

"Don't. She's not hurting me, and maybe she just wants a handle to hold onto. After all, she's quite a few feet off the ground. I'd want something to hold on to as well."

Holding the baby brought back all the yearnings Lana had harbored before she'd married Mason. If everything had gone according to plans, she would have been holding her own baby in her arms at that moment.

The smell of baby shampoo and baby powder filled Lana's senses, hitting her square in her womb. She wanted a child of her own. More than that, she wanted a man who loved her and would do anything for her. Was it too much to ask?

"Please, come inside." Sadie opened the screen

door at the front of the house and held it for Lana to enter with Emma. "The mosquitos come out at night in droves, and it's starting to get dark."

She sighed and held baby Emma close as she passed through the door into the spacious ranch house. Maybe it would be enough if she just borrowed Sadie's baby any time she felt that maternal instinct rear its demanding head.

With a killer out to get her, she had no business bringing a child into the world.

Emma grinned and made a grab for Lana's hair again.

She didn't mind when the baby curled her little fingers around a long, thick strand.

Holding Emma made her realize two things. She had to resolve the killer situation, and she wanted what Sadie had.

Not the fame and fortune, but the husband and family Lana craved so much.

CHAPTER 9

ALL THROUGH DINNER with the Pattersons, Trevor couldn't tear his gaze off Lana. She held baby Emma throughout the meal, playing with her and talking to her as if she were one of the adults at the table.

Lana was a natural with babies. She needed to have some of her own.

That thought led to the next.

What would Lana's babies look like? Would she have little girls with long, straight, sandy-blond hair like their mother's, or would she have little boys with dark brown hair and brown eyes? Boys who looked like him.

Holy shit! What was he thinking? He couldn't give Lana babies. She was Mason's widow. Since Mason was like a brother to Trevor, making love to his widow would be like making love to his sister, wouldn't it?

But he wanted to be the father of Lana's children as much as he wanted to be the one and only love of her life.

For years, he'd told himself he never wanted to marry. Marriage was hard. But when you were a Navy SEAL, deployed more than you were home, it was doubly difficult. He'd seen so many of his buddies' relationships end in divorce.

"You're staying with us tonight, aren't you?" Sadie asked out of the blue, pulling Trevor back to the table and the conversation going on around him.

Trevor shook his head automatically. "We're staying at the bed and breakfast where I've rented a room for the month."

Lana shot a glance his way but didn't refute what he'd said.

She would probably be safer at the White Oak Ranch surrounded by Hank's security system.

"Remind me to engage a local realtor in finding you a more permanent home in Eagle Rock." Hank touched a hand to Trevor's arm. "I'm worried about the two of you. Do you think you'll be safe in the B&B?"

Trevor caught Lana's gaze and held it. "If you feel safer here at Hank's place, you should stay." It would be the right thing to do. But Trevor wanted to be with her. She was his responsibility. He'd promised Mason. More than that, he wanted to be the one looking out for Lana.

Lana shook her head slowly and then turned to Hank and Sadie. "Thank you...but I think I'll stay with Trevor. He's gotten me this far. I feel safe with him."

Hank smiled. "You're both welcome to stay here, if you want Trevor to provide for your safety."

Lana gave Sadie a smile that reminded Trevor of why he loved this woman so much. "I'd rather go to the B&B where Trevor lives. I've imposed enough on your hospitality."

Sadie waved a dismissive hand. "Oh, Lana. You haven't imposed on anything. And Emma loves you already."

Halfway through the meal, the baby had fallen asleep in Lana's arms.

Lana laughed. "Seems I have a knack with babies. My friends back in San Diego all ask me to hold their little ones. They must think I'm comfortable, because they all fall asleep while I'm holding them."

Sadie smiled. "You need babies of your own, Lana."

Lana shook her head. "Not until I'm out of danger. I couldn't bear to put a child in harm's way."

Sadie's lips twisted. "Do you hear that Hank? You need to make sure our Lana is safe, and that the danger she's facing now is contained."

Hank grinned at his wife. "Yes, ma'am. I think the FBI is on the case."

"That doesn't mean you can't check into things to

assist the FBI in wrapping it up as soon as possible." Sadie gave her husband a raised eyebrow. "Lana can't live in fear for too long. She has a life to live."

Trevor liked how Sadie believed her husband could accomplish anything. He'd had the idea that once they turned the files over to the FBI, they could retire to Montana and let the Feds do their magic in solving the case.

But the more he thought about it, the more he realized the FBI might not resolve the issues quickly enough.

The Feds could take days, weeks or even months to track down all the leads Lana had provided.

"Hank, you have a computer guy on the team, don't you?" Trevor asked.

His boss nodded. "That would be Axel Svenson or Swede, as we like to call him. He's got a talent for hacking into systems."

Trevor turned to Lana. "We'll set up a time tomorrow to meet with Swede. Maybe he can come at the data from a different angle and pinpoint the guys who are up to their eyeballs in treason."

"He usually comes in around nine in the morning. You're welcome to bring what you have and work with him in my offices."

"Thanks. We will." Trevor pushed back from the table. "I can help clean up, but afterward, we need to get to town. I know I'm beat, and I'm sure Lana is, too."

Lana nodded and rose from the table with Emma in her arms. "Where should I lay her down?"

Sadie rose from her seat. "If you want, I can take her."

"No need. Just point me in the right direction."

After Sadie gave her directions to Emma's room, Lana disappeared.

Trevor carried his plate into the kitchen and rinsed it off in the sink.

Sadie and Hank carried more dishes in.

"You don't have to worry about the dishes. Hank and I have a system," Sadie gave her husband a sweet smile. "He washes. I dry."

Hank kissed his wife and pulled her into his arms. "Or we rinse and put them in the dishwasher, and take advantage of the fact Emma is asleep..."

Sadie laughed. "I like your idea." She gave Trevor a quick glance. "We've got the dishes covered if you and Lana want to escape."

Hank dug into his pocket and then held out a hand, without releasing his wife.

Trevor reached for the hand, intending to shake it, but Hank dropped a set of keys into his palm. "Take my truck. Use it as long as you need it."

"Thanks," Trevor said. "We'll be back in the morning to work with Swede. I can drop it off then."

"I'll let Swede know to expect you." Hank returned his attention to his beautiful wife.

Trevor backed out of the kitchen. "We'll let ourselves out."

Hank nuzzled his wife's neck. "Umm. Great."

Trevor turned away, not wanting to intrude on the couple's intimacy. His heart tugged hard in his chest. He found himself wishing he could have the open, unfettered relationship Hank and Sadie enjoyed.

He wished he could have it with Lana.

All those years as a young Navy SEAL, he thought he didn't want to get married. He hadn't wanted to get married because he hadn't found the right woman. Until Lana.

Following the directions Sadie had given Lana, Trevor found her leaning over a baby crib, singing softly to Emma. Her voice was soft, melodic and so beautiful it made Trevor's eyes sting and knot form in his throat. He loved this woman.

Surely, Mason would understand if Trevor wooed and married his widow. She deserved to be happy, to have a family with babies to raise. She'd make an incredible mother.

Trevor decided at that moment to do everything in his power to woo and marry this woman. He'd missed his chance once. He wouldn't miss it again.

But he'd have to take it slowly. Mason's death and the subsequent investigation had consumed Lana for over a year. His challenge was to help her to see past her loss to a potential future with him.

With that goal in mind, Trevor cleared his throat softly.

Lana's head jerked up, and she pressed a finger to her lips. Still in her sing-song voice, she said, "She's not quite asleep, but soon, little baby. Soon you'll float in the clouds and close your little eyes." She crooned to Emma until the child's eyes fluttered closed, and she slept.

Lana tiptoed to the door and paused, glancing back at the crib to make certain Emma was truly asleep. Then she took Trevor's hand and walked out into the living room.

She started for the kitchen when Trevor brought her up short. Lana gave him a puzzled look. "I want to thank the Pattersons for dinner."

"They were busy."

"Well, I can help with the dishes." She started for the kitchen again.

Again, Trevor held her back. "They're busy- busy."

"What do you mean, busy-busy?"

He winked. "They want to be alone."

Lana's eyes rounded. "Oh. Okay."

"I told them we'd show ourselves out." He headed for the foyer and the front door of the ranch house, eager to get Lana alone in his room, away from everyone else. Not that he'd seduce her. But he wanted to show her how much he cared and that they were good together. How he'd do that, he wasn't sure, but having her to himself was a start.

. . .

WITH HER HAND held firmly in Trevor's, Lana walked out onto the porch and stared up at the huge Montana sky full of sparkling stars. "Oh, my. Look at all the stars." She hugged his arm. "I can see why you love it here."

"That's one thing I didn't care for in San Diego. You have to get way out of the city to see the stars. The city lights shine too bright to enjoy stargazing there."

"True. I'm glad you brought me here." She kept pace with him as he descended the porch steps and crossed to the truck Hank had loaned him. "I wouldn't have felt secure staying in my house in San Diego."

"You're with me, now. I'll do my best to keep you safe."

Again, she hugged his arm. "Thanks, Trevor. You've always had a special place in my heart."

"I might not have shown you often enough, but you've always had top billing in mine."

Lana's pulse thundered through her veins. What did that mean? Did Trevor love her? And if so, was it like a sister, or a lover?

Lana forced herself to be calm. His comment was that of a true friend. She couldn't read more into it than that. Not yet. Mason was gone. She hadn't died with him. It was time she moved on with the rest of her life. And she wanted Trevor in it. Of that, she was absolutely certain.

She sat in the front seat of the truck, hands in her lap, eyes looking forward through the entire drive into Eagle Rock.

When they arrived at the B&B, she didn't wait for Trevor to open her door, but got down by herself and met him in on the sidewalk in front of an old single-family mansion that had been converted into lodging for many.

What she could see from the light burning on the porch was a gingerbread design with blue-gray paint and white trim. The windows had flowerboxes full of bright pink petunias, drooping over the edges. The garden was filled with bushes and colorful annuals. Someone took pride in the place. It had a warm, welcoming atmosphere that made Lana glad she came.

Trevor opened the front door for her and ushered her into a common area strewn with comfortable chairs and sofas. At one end was a dining room with small tables and a coffeemaker in the corner.

He led her up a sweeping staircase to a hallway with many doors.

At the second one on the right, he inserted a key in the lock, twisted and pushed the door open.

Inside was a room straight out of the nineteenth century, with a white iron bed covered in an old quilt and layered with fluffy pillows.

An antique dresser took up one wall and a small floral sofa rested against the other.

Lana's heart beat faster. "Do they have another room? Or are we both sleeping in this one?"

"I'm pretty sure they don't have any more rooms available and definitely not one adjoining this one with a door between." He kicked the door closed behind him and locked it. "After what happened in San Diego, I don't want you too far out of my sight."

She nodded. "Agreed." Still her heart hammered against her ribs at the possibilities of sharing such a small room with Trevor.

"Don't worry," he said. "I'll sleep on the couch. You can have the bed."

"Oh. Okay," she said, her pulse skidding to a halt and resuming to a more sedate beat. Why had she thought he'd share his bed with her? They were friends, not lovers. That one kiss they'd shared so long ago hadn't meant nearly as much to him as it had to her. She closed her eyes. Perhaps, for him, that kiss had cemented the fact they should remain friends. He might not have felt the same spark of electricity as she had.

"The bathroom is small, but it does have a shower and extra sample bottles of shampoo."

Lana sighed. "I had all of that in the suitcase we left in the back of the rental car. I hope the police or FBI keep my bag for me." She patted her purse. "At least I carry my brush with me. But I have no clothing to change into."

Trevor dug in a drawer and pulled out a soft gray T-shirt. "Will this work for something to sleep in?"

She nodded. "And I can rinse the clothes I have on and hang them up to dry. But tomorrow, I need to do some shopping."

"Deal." Trevor handed her the shirt, and their knuckles brushed.

Lana felt that charge of awareness like a shock from an electric fence. She glanced up to see if Trevor had the same experience.

If he had, he wasn't showing it. His face was a mask with no emotions reflected.

"You can have the shower first," he offered. "I'll go see if I can scrounge some tea. You still like hot tea at night, don't you?"

She nodded, pleased that he'd remembered. "Thank you."

With the T-shirt in hand, she let herself into the bathroom and closed the door behind her. Then she stripped out of her clothing, turned on the water and started to draw the curtain around the antique claw-foot tub, but stopped.

How often did she get to take a bath in a claw-foot tub? It appeared too inviting to pass up. Beside the tub was an array of shampoos and homemade soaps and bath salts.

Lana shoved the plug into the drain and filled the

tub with warm water. Then she slid into the water, going under long enough to wet her hair. She used one of the scented shampoos to thoroughly clean her hair. Ducking beneath the surface of the water again, she rinsed the soap out and came up for air.

She squeezed the moisture out of her hair and piled it up on top of her head. Then she sprinkled bath salts into the water and let the oils and scents surround her. This was heaven. Pure heaven.

She lay back against the porcelain rim and closed her eyes. After all she'd been through, this made up for much of it.

The only thing that could make it better was if Trevor joined her.

At the mere thought, her body heated, her core coiled into a deliciously tight knot and her sex ached.

By now, he'd be back with that cup of tea, waiting only steps away on the other side of the door.

All she had to do was ask him to come in.

Lana opened her mouth to do just that, but clamped her lips shut before she got up the courage.

She told herself that if he were interested, he'd have made a move by now.

On the other hand, he might be acting chivalrous and consider the widow of his dead buddy off-limits. In which case, she could kiss goodbye any chance of making love with Trevor Anderson.

The water was starting to cool by the time she rose from the scented water. She stepped out of the tub, pulled the drain plug and dried her body. Pulling the T-shirt over her head, she laughed when it came down to her knees. A glance in the mirror confirmed. She looked like a little girl, her curves swallowed by the gray blob of a shirt.

Why did she care? It wasn't as if she was going to seduce the man. Most definitely not while dressed in the T-shirt. Leaning over, she wrapped her wet hair in the towel and flipped it up, turban-style. She quickly rinsed her panties in the sink and hung them on the towel rod to dry. Her shirt and jeans would have to last another day until she could find a store to purchase additional clothing.

Satisfied she looked like a waif and as unsexy as she could possibly get, she stepped out of the bathroom wearing the baggy shirt and nothing else. That she wore no panties made her hyper-aware of every move. Jersey fabric brushed against her thighs and buttocks as a constant reminder of her nakedness beneath the long shirt.

Her breathing grew ragged, and her pulse raced out of control.

Trevor stood in the middle of the room with a cup of tea in his hand. "Feel better?" He handed her the tea and nodded toward the couch. "Have a sip. Then I want to talk about how we're going to keep you safe."

So nervous, she couldn't think straight, she

gulped the hot tea, burning her tongue. Lana sputtered and stuck her tongue out to cool.

"Sorry, I forgot to tell you it was really hot." He patted her back, took the teacup from her hand and pressed a glass of ice water in its place.

She sipped on the icy cold liquid, letting it run across her scalded tongue. The hot tea really hadn't burned that badly, but she was nervous and didn't know what else to say, or what to do with her hands.

Trevor took the ice water from her hands and set it on the nightstand. "Now, I wanted to talk about your defense."

"Defense?" she squeaked, cleared her throat and tried again. "Defense?"

"Yes. If I'm not always around—which I intend to be—you need to know a few basic moves to defend yourself."

"I've taken a self-defense course, if that's what you're talking about."

"Good. Then show me what you have."

Her heart skipped several beats as thoughts of her panty-less bottom were conjured by his words. She loosened the towel on her head and flung it across the footboard of the bed. Her hair hung down her back in long damp tresses. She didn't care. She had to prove to Trevor she wasn't completely defenseless.

Trevor turned her to where her back faced him. "What would you do if someone came up behind you and grabbed you around the neck like this?" He hooked her neck with his elbow.

Lana grabbed where his hands connected, twisted her head to the side, while pulling down on his arms and ducked beneath his elbow. She spun to face him and lifted her foot to plant her heel in his groin.

He blocked her kick and chuckled. "Well done." He advanced on her before she realized what he was doing and pinned her wrists to the wall. "Now, what are you going to do?" he said, his face so close to her she could feel the warmth of his breath on her cheeks.

Her muscles turned to mush, and her knees threatened to buckle. Her gaze met his, and for a long moment, she forgot how to breathe. Then she leaned forward and pressed her lips to his.

CHAPTER 10

TREVOR NEVER EXPECTED Lana's reaction to being pinned to the wall. When her lips touched his, he couldn't remember what point he was trying to make. All he could think about was how soft, warm and delicious her mouth felt against his.

He leaned into the kiss and skimmed his tongue across her lips.

Lana gasped, her teeth parting enough Trevor thrust past them to caress her tongue in a long, sensuous stroke. He released her wrists and cupped the back of her head, his fingers threaded into her damp hair, and he pulled her closer, until their bodies pressed chest to chest and hip to hip.

His groin swelled, his cock nudging her belly. God, he wanted more. When she wrapped her arms around his neck and deepened the kiss, he placed his hands around the backs of her thighs and scooped her up.

Lana wrapped her legs around his waist and locked her ankles behind him. The T-shirt rode up her thighs, exposing her bare bottom to his grasp.

A moan rose up Trevor's throat. Sweet heaven, she was naked beneath the shirt. All his good intentions of taking it slow with her flew out the window as her center rubbed against the fly of his jeans.

He dragged his mouth away from hers and kissed a path along her chin to suck at her earlobe. "Say the word, and I stop right here."

"Please," she said.

He held his breath, prepared to end it on her command.

"Don't stop," she whispered, her voice ragged, her hands guiding his head back to kiss her again.

"I couldn't if I tried." And he dove in to claim her mouth in a kiss that shattered him. When he came back to reality, he'd pick up the pieces and assemble a new person. But for now, he was all hers, and she was his.

Without taking his mouth from hers, he carried her to the bed and let her legs slide down the sides of his thighs until her feet touched the floor.

She stepped back and stared up into his eyes. Then, without blinking, she grabbed the hem of her shirt and pulled it up over her head, tossing it to the corner.

Trevor's body lit like a flame to gasoline.

Lana was every bit as beautiful on the outside as she was on the inside. Her breasts were small but perfectly shaped and firm. The indentation of her tiny waist emphasized the swell of her hips. The soft ruff of blond hair at the apex of her thighs beckoned Trevor.

He groaned and reached for the buttons on his shirt, his fingers fumbling to release them. At the very moment he decided to rip the shirt off his back, she covered his hands and took over.

One at a time, she released the buttons, moving downward to where the shirt disappeared into the waistband of his jeans. Her fingers flicked open the button on his jeans and eased the zipper down.

Trevor's cock sprang free, hard and straight, filling her palm.

He was going commando.

She wrapped her hand around his staff and ran it from the tip to the base then paused to fondle his balls. Then she pushed his jeans down his hips and dropped to her knees to ease the denim over his thighs and calves.

Trevor toed off his shoes and stepped free of them and his jeans. He released the last buttons on his shirt and shucked it over his shoulders, letting it drop to the floor.

Still on her knees, Lana touched her tongue to the tip of his cock and swirled around the tiny hole at the center. She widened her circles to lick around the rim of his head, again and again.

Trevor dug his fingers into her hair and held her there, his head flung back, his breath barely filling his lungs.

Lana took him into her mouth, gripped his ass and drove him all the way in until he bumped the back of her throat.

Trevor couldn't breathe, couldn't move. This woman was amazing. He hadn't started the day thinking anything like this could happen but thank the heavens it had.

She guided him in and out, settling into a steady rhythm, moving faster and faster until it was all Trevor could do to keep from coming in her mouth. He gripped her head and pulled free, then drew her up into his arms where he kissed her. The taste of him on her lips nearly made him lose control.

After several deep, calming breaths, he scooped her up in his arms and laid her on the bed.

She parted her legs, and he climbed between them, stopping short when he remembered.

He climbed off the bed and dove for his jeans and the wallet in the back pocket.

"What?" Lana leaned up on one elbow. "What's wrong?"

He fumbled in his wallet, praying he'd find what he was searching for. When his hand wrapped around the little foil packet, he held it up triumphantly. "Protection."

She dropped back on the bed, a chuckle rocking her body. "I'm glad one of us is thinking."

He climbed onto the bed between her legs and brushed his lips across hers.

Taking the condom from his fingers, she tore it open and rolled it over his erection, her fingers lingering at the base.

Then she raised her knees and guided him to her center.

"Wait," he said.

She let go of a long, slow breath. "What now?"

"You're not there yet."

"I'm so close I could die," she whispered and brought his face down to hers for another kiss.

"But you're not there." He left her lips and trailed kisses down the side of her neck to the pulse pounding at the base of her throat. But he didn't stop there. He continued downward, took a nipple between his teeth and rolled it until it hardened into a tight knot.

Her back arched off the bed and she moaned.

He switched to the other breast and treated it to the same pleasure, reveling in the way she writhed beneath him.

Eager to bring her the rest of the way there, he kissed and tongued a path down her torso to the tuft of hair guarding her sex. There he parted her folds and dragged a finger from her damp entrance up to that knot of nerve-packed flesh.

Lana tensed, her hips rising off the mattress. "Oh, Trevor. Please."

"Please what?"

"More, please," she whispered.

He replaced his finger with his tongue and licked that nubbin until she gripped his hair in her fingers and held him close, her hips rocking, her fingernails digging into his scalp.

He knew when she came by the way her body froze, and her back stiffened. Still, he didn't let up, wanting her to ride that wave all the way to the end.

When she relaxed against the comforter, he climbed up her body and pressed the tip of his cock against her entrance. "Still with me?"

She shook her head. "I'm somewhere up there in the heavens."

"Want me to stop?"

"Oh, hell no." She clutched his ass in her palms and brought him home.

He glided into her slick channel, burying himself all the way to the hilt.

Lana wrapped her legs around him and dug her heels into his buttocks, forcing him even deeper.

Then he was pumping in and out of her, harder, faster until every nerve in his body burned with his desire, and he shot over the edge.

One final thrust brought him as close as he could

get to Lana. He stayed deep inside her until the spasms of his release waned and he could breathe normally again.

He dropped down on top of her and rolled them to the side, retaining their intimate connection.

For a long time, they lay in each other's arms until Trevor's breathing returned to normal and sleep tugged at his eyelids.

Trevor pulled free and disposed of the condom. Then he drew her back into his embrace. "About that defensive move..." He pressed a kiss to her forehead. "Amazing."

She smiled and kissed his chin. "Told you I could take care of myself." Lana yawned and snuggled closer, her breasts pressed against his chest.

Trevor pulled the blanket over them and promptly fell asleep, basking in the glow of the best sex he'd ever had. He refused to believe they ended here. If it was the last thing he did, he'd make Lana fall in love with him. Then he'd marry her and get on with the happily-ever-after part of life with Lana.

CHAPTER 11

LANA WOKE to sunlight streaming through the window. Memories of the night before rushed back into her mind and warmed her all over.

Wow. Had she really made love with Trevor? She moved, touching herself down there. Oh, yes. Deliciously sore, she'd made love to the man and she had no regrets.

But the pillow beside her was empty. A sound in the bathroom made her turn her head in time to find Trevor shaved, dressed and smiling down at her. "Mrs. Kinner serves breakfast from seven until nine. It's eight, and I'm starving."

"So, you want me to get moving?" She stretched, letting the blanket slide down her body, exposing her breasts. "Are you sure you're hungry for food?"

Trevor groaned and dropped down on the bed beside her to take one of her nipples into his mouth.

He flicked the tip with his tongue and nipped lightly. "Ummm. You're tempting. I'd say to hell with breakfast, but we're supposed to meet with Swede at nine."

Lana sighed. "Such a shame to waste a perfectly good morning working."

"Can't do much more without a resupply. I only had one condom in my wallet. Remind me to stop at the store on the way back." He dropped a kiss on her forehead. "That is, of course, if you're still interested in more lessons on self-defense." He slapped her naked bottom and yanked the quilt off her. "Up, lady. This bear is hungry."

"Pushy bastard, aren't you?" she grumbled, but rolled to her feet and walked naked into the bathroom, making sure to use her runway walk, swinging her hips side to side enough to drive any man wild.

Before she crossed the threshold of the bathroom, big hands landed on her hips and pulled her back against a hard chest and an equally hard erection.

"Woman, you're testing me."

"And you're passing with flying colors." She turned in his arms and pressed her breasts to his chest and her lips to his in a brief kiss. Then she backed away quickly and shut the door. "I'll be ready in two shakes," she called out.

TREVOR ADJUSTED his jeans to ease the strain on his cock and marveled at how quickly they'd gone from friends to lovers. He'd worried there would be a lot of awkwardness between them when Lana woke. He'd second-guessed making love to her the night before. Not that he regretted it. He just didn't want to ruin his chances of keeping Lana in his life. Of having and holding her until death do they part.

Yeah, he was head-over-heels for the woman. Just like he'd been before she'd married Mason. Nothing had changed, except he loved her even more.

Moments later, Lana appeared in the clothes she'd worn the day before, her hair neatly pulled back in a loose ponytail. Fresh-cheeked, she looked like a teenager, all sunshine and carefree.

"Will Mrs. Kinner be mad that you had a guest in your room last night?" she whispered as they exited the room and locked the door.

"She's really nice. I'm sure she won't mind."

"Good. I don't want to get you kicked out of your room. Eagle Rock can't have too many options, as small as it is."

"You're right. There aren't many options. I think they have a couple of rooms over the Blue Moose Tavern. Other than that, I'm not sure who else runs a bed and breakfast, and there aren't any hotels."

"I'll be really nice to Mrs. Kinner," Lana promised.

Mrs. Kinner was welcoming and happy to meet Lana. She offered to cook anything she wanted for breakfast.

Lana chose to have a piece of toast and a boiled egg.

Trevor ordered bacon, eggs, hash browns and toast.

Mrs. Kinner disappeared into the kitchen and reappeared fifteen minutes later with their food.

After breakfast, Trevor checked outside the B&B for trouble. When he was certain there weren't any bad guys lurking in the shadows, he allowed Lana to leave the building and climb up into Hank's truck.

For the first few minutes of the drive, Lana sat quietly in her seat, staring at the road ahead. Once they left town, she turned toward Trevor. "Do you think Mason would be mad about us?"

Trevor had wondered that himself. "Mason wouldn't have asked me to take care of you, if he didn't want me to be with you."

"Do you feel guilty at all about what we did? I mean, when it comes to Mason." Lana twisted her fingers together in her lap, her gaze on her hands.

"Mason would've wanted us to get on with our lives, Lana. I don't feel guilty about what happened last night. I'm kind of thankful it did."

"Thankful?" Lana finally turned toward him, a frown wrinkling her brow. "Why?"

"I sense that neither of us was surprised about what happened. Am I right?" he asked.

Lana opened her mouth, closed it and nodded.

"Don't get me wrong. I loved Mason with all my heart."

"I know," Trevor responded softly. "So did I. He was my best friend."

"And mine. We were The Three Musketeers."

"Until there were two," Trevor added.

"And you backed away." She looked out her window, her face turned away but reflected in the glass. "I missed you."

"I missed you both," Trevor admitted. "I felt like I'd lost my two best friends."

"But we were still there."

"Yeah, but everything had changed."

"I don't regret marrying Mason. He was an amazing man, and a caring husband. I regret that it ruined our friendship."

"If nothing else comes of us," Trevor said. "I hope we can always be friends."

"You can count on it. Keep your friends close and your best friends closer." She smiled across at him and held out her hand.

He took it and squeezed gently. Life had gotten so much better in the last twenty-four hours.

Lana was back in his life.

Trevor turned into the gate at the White Oak Ranch. He punched in the code, and the gate opened automatically.

The driveway wove between trees and around curves all the way up to the sprawling ranch house on a knoll looking out over a stunning stretch of the Crazy Mountains.

"I could learn to love this place," Lana said. "The views are spectacular."

Shifting into park, Trevor leaned across the cab and pressed a quick kiss to Lana's lips. "We should talk this evening."

"I'm all for some more self-defense lessons." Lana winked. "Or we can talk."

He gave her a quick smile. "Let's go see what Swede can come up with."

"I doubt he'll get more than my dude on the dark web. But he might know some tricks neither of us has tried."

Lana hefted her bag onto her shoulder and followed Trevor up the porch steps.

Hank greeted them at the door. "Sadie had to go into Eagle Rock for a few things at the store. She took Emma with her." He showed them into the house. "Trevor's been to my bunker before, but this will be a new experience for you, Lana." He pressed his thumb to a scanner on a wall between the kitchen and living room. A moment later, a door slid open, and a light blinked on in a stairwell descending into a bunker below the house.

"Wow," Lana said. "And I thought this was a cool house before I knew it had a bunker beneath it."

Hank led the way down the steps and into a room lined with computers. A blond-haired man sat in front of one of them. When they entered, he rose from his chair and seemed to brush the ceiling with the top of his head. He was so tall and broad-shouldered he made big men like Hank and Trevor look short next to him.

Hank waved toward the big guy. "Swede, this is Lana Connolly. Her husband was Con Man Connolly, that Navy SEAL who died last year on a mission in Afghanistan."

Swede's brow furrowed. "Sorry for your loss. I heard about that on the news." He turned to Trevor. "You were there, weren't you?"

Trevor nodded. "Connolly was one of our best."

Swede nodded and returned his focus to Lana. "Hank said you've done some digging into what was going on back then and came up with some rotten potatoes."

Her lips twitched. "You could call them that." She pulled her laptop out of her purse and set it on the table beside the computer Swede was using. "I started all this because the doctor who pronounced my husband said he was shot in the back."

"Friendly fire?" Swede asked.

"Or not so friendly," Lana said. "I found out the contractor working with government money to help rebuild Afghan infrastructure wasn't using the money the way he should. He was funneling it back to the States. He and a director in Homeland Security deposited the funds into a secret bank account in the Cayman Islands."

"Why didn't you turn it all over to the FBI when you found out about it?"

She pressed her lips together. "I couldn't. My information was from a source on the dark web. I couldn't hand over my data. It wouldn't have been considered legitimate. And it might have led to exposing my contact on the dark web.

"So, I went to work for the DHS where this director worked, hoping to get into his systems there and find some legitimate evidence I could turn over to the FBI."

"And did you?"

Lana nodded. "I worked with a colleague on the inside and dug up some emails I think were pretty damning. They pointed to an organization in the Bitterroot Mountains of Montana that, on the surface, looks like a construction company. After a little digging and following some leads provided by my hacker, I discovered this group in Montana has connections to a social media group called Free America. They're encouraging people to stage a coup to overthrow the US government."

Swede took his seat at the table and rested his fingers on the keyboard. "So, the money from the contracts in Afghanistan is going to Cayman banks, and you think it's finding its way into the coffers of this militant group...?"

"Yes. I turned over everything, except my dark web connection, to the FBI yesterday. They said they'd look into it."

"So, tell me about the contractor in Afghanistan and work your way through everything you've found. I'll take notes." Swede brought up a blank document and started keying in the data Lana provided.

While Lana and Swede talked, Hank took Trevor into the arms room of his bunker.

"I'm worried about Lana. Based on the number of attacks and the intensity of their determination to kill her, I don't think they'll give up just because she left the state." Hank pulled out a drawer filled with electronic gadgets. "I think it would be a good idea to put a tracker on her. If she gets...misplaced, you'll find her."

Trevor liked the idea. "As long as the tracker remains with her. What are the choices? It would have to be something she'd always carry with her, something that doesn't scream *tracker*."

Hank smiled. "I have just the thing." He dug a small case out of the box and handed it to Trevor. "Give it to her like a gift. She'll never know she's being tracked."

Trevor frowned. "Wouldn't she feel safer knowing?"

"Then give her one to put in her pocket. If she gets separated from her pocket, you can be sure she's still wearing any gift you give her. It's waterproof, so it can be submerged and can be worn in the shower. Tell her she can wear it at all times."

Trevor flipped open the box and stared at the gold necklace. He liked this idea, and the necklace was nice enough he would have given it to her anyway. "Thank you."

"Oh, we're not done yet. You might need some fire-power in case you get into a shootout again with this guy." He opened a cabinet with a display of handguns. "Pick your poison. And take a shoulder holster as well."

Trevor selected a Sig P226 and the holster to carry it.

"Get a knife as well."

"I have my Ka-Bar from my Navy SEAL days. It'll do."

"Good." Hank moved onto another cabinet with smaller devices. He pulled out what appeared to be a small, pink, handheld flashlight with a wrist strap and handed it to Trevor. "Give this to Lana."

He weighed it in his hand, studying it. "Stun gun?"

"Yup. I got one for Sadie for her birthday. She carries it on her wrist when she's out at night in LA."

"Good idea. It's not going to go off on me if I put it in my pocket, is it?"

Hank laughed. "No. You have to activate it before it'll work. We can show Lana how to use it before you two leave today. I'd offer her a gun, but I don't know if she's familiar with firing one, and she probably doesn't have a conceal carry permit."

"We can ask when she's done with Swede."

"What do you want to ask?" Lana appeared in the doorway. "Swede's off and running with what I gave him. What are you two cooking up in here?" She glanced at the racks of rifles and handguns and let out a long, low whistle. "Wow. You know how to stock an arsenal. Should the US government be worried?"

Hank shook his head. "I don't expect my guys to provide protection without options."

"Nice to know." Lana raised her brow. "Am I to assume you're packing?"

Trevor nodded and opened his jacket to display the P226 nestled in the holster there. "Hank said he'd offer you one if you want."

She shook her head. "Guns scare me. If I had time to learn how to use one, maybe. But for now, I'll rely on my self-defense lessons." Her lips curled, and she shot Trevor a sassy smile.

He held out the stun gun. "You can at least carry this on your person, should you need a little help subduing an attacker."

Lana stared down at the stun gun. "Is that what I think it is?"

"If you think it's a stun gun, then yes." Trevor smiled. "Hank will show you how to use it."

In a few quick, easy steps, Hank showed Lana how to activate the stun gun.

When they were done, Lana sighed. "As much as I enjoy your company, Hank, I'd really like a change of clothes." Her gaze met Trevor's. "Could we make a run into town?"

"Hank, could you give us a lift into town?" Trevor asked. "That way you can keep your truck. Mine is still at the Blue Moose Tavern. I can pick it up from there."

"Sure. Let me get my hat." Hank led the way out of the bunker and shut the door behind them. "I'll be right back."

Lana palmed the stun gun. "I hope I don't have to use this. Most likely, I'll end up zapping myself instead of the bad guy."

"You'll be okay. Better to have it than to be defenseless."

"Oh, I have moves," Lana said and stepped up to Trevor.

"I remember." He dropped a kiss on her lips and stepped away as footsteps sounded on the wood floors.

"Ready?" Hank plunked his cowboy hat onto his head and jerked his head toward the door. "I might even meet my wife in town for lunch."

The three of them walked out to Hank's truck. Lana insisted on sitting in the back where she turned the stun gun over and over in her hand.

Hank talked about some of the assignments his men were getting and how business was booming. He had a new guy signed up to cover assignments on the east coast, working out of Cape Cod.

Trevor remembered John Decker's name. He'd never served with him, but he'd heard the guy was one of the best of the Navy SEALs on SEAL Team 10. The man had lost his wife in a terrible accident.

The thought of losing Lana made Trevor's gut bunch into a knot. Losing Mason had been hard enough. The man had been like a brother. If he lost Lana…he wasn't sure how he'd carry on.

So, he had to make sure she was safe, and he didn't lose her. She was his everything. Staying away from her for the past two years had nearly killed him.

It was noon by the time they pulled up in front of the Blue Moose Tavern. Sadie and Emma met them out front.

Lana spent a few minutes playing with the baby before she excused herself and joined Trevor. "I really need to get some clothes. If you want to stay and have lunch with the Pattersons, I can manage shopping on my own. No one will bother me in broad daylight." She held up the stun gun. "And I have this in case someone steps out of line."

"I'm going with you."

She rolled her eyes. "Seriously, I don't need you to babysit me every hour of every day. I need time to try on bras and purchase panties. Do you want to stand in the lingerie department while I'm doing that?"

"I don't care what department I have to stand in. I'm going with you," he insisted. The fresh thought of losing her made him even more adamant.

Lana shrugged. "Suit yourself. But you were warned."

She turned to Sadie and asked about local clothes shopping.

"There isn't much here in Eagle Rock. You might have to drive into Bozeman if you want more than jeans and flannel shirts."

Lana's gaze met Trevor's.

He grinned and held up his truck keys. "Guess you're stuck with me."

"You can loan me your truck and I can go by myself," she suggested.

"And miss the fashion show?" He winked and hooked her arm. "Not on your life." Over his shoulder, he said, "See ya later, Hank. Good to see you, Sadie. Give Emma a kiss from Uncle Trevor."

Hank and Sadie laughed and waved.

Trevor led Lana to where his truck was parked and held the door open while she slid into the passenger seat.

"Most men hate shopping," Lana said.

"Normally, I do, too. But if shopping means I get to see you in lace bras and underwear, I'm in." He grinned and waggled his eyebrows.

She waved a finger at him. "Forget it. You won't be in the changing room with me."

"You mean, you won't be modeling your lingerie for me?" He pouted. For a big guy, the pout was pretty darned cute.

"No." She relented. "But if you play your cards right, I might model them for you tonight."

Trevor closed her door, rounded the front of the truck and opened the driver's door. He grabbed a cowboy hat off the back of the seat and settled it on his head.

Lana grinned. "I don't ever recall seeing you wear a cowboy hat."

"You've never been to Montana with me."

"Do you even know what a cow is?" she asked.

"Know them and have worked with them growing up. And I ride like nobody's business. Used to bust broncs in the rodeo when I was a teen. Won the teen state championship once."

Lana stared at him as if for the first time. "I did not know that."

"It didn't seem important, living in San Diego where all you have is sun, sand and ocean. Here in Montana, we have mountains, plains, horses, cattle, bears and wolves."

Lana's brows dipped. "Bears and wolves?" She glanced around the small town. "Bears and wolves?"

"Yeah." He grinned. "Rethinking Hank's offer of a gun to carry on you?"

"Damn right."

"Don't worry. They usually don't bother people. Unless you get between a mama and her cubs."

"Remind me not to get between a mama and her cubs." Lana shivered. "What is this place you've brought me to?"

"The best state in the union." He pulled out of the parking lot and onto the highway they'd come in on the night before.

As they left town, Trevor reached into the pocket in his jacket and extracted the long, slim jewelry box Hank had given him. "Got a little gift for you. Actually, Sadie had it and thought you might like it. Though I'd really like to take credit for it, I can't." Trevor congratulated himself on the little white lie about Sadie suggesting the necklace instead of Hank.

"Thanks...I think." She opened the box and stared down at the necklace inside. "This is really pretty."

"You had to leave all of your things behind in the rental car. Sadie and I thought you might like a little something pretty to go with the clothes you buy today."

"That was nice of her. Remind me to thank her next time we see her." Lana took the necklace out of the box and fastened it around her neck. The pretty gray-blue stone pendant matched the color of Lana's eyes. "Beautiful," Trevor said.

Lana's cheeks flushed a pretty pink. "Thank you. It was really nice of Sadie."

"She said it's waterproof. You can wear it all the time. Even in the shower."

"That's great. I don't always remember to remove jewelry when I jump into the shower." She lowered the visor and stared at her reflection in the mirror.

Trevor took that moment to dig the other little metal tracking device out of his pocket. "And Hank sent this."

Lana held out her hand out, palm up. "What is it?"

"It's a tracker," he said, placing it on her open hand. "As long as you have this on your person, I can track you. If someone should snatch you away from me, I'll be able to find you."

Lana stared from the tiny metal object to Trevor, and her eyes shone with unshed tears. "That's about the nicest gift anyone has ever given me."

Trevor shot her a confused glance. "Really?"

"This gift tells me you're all worried about me." She smiled at him through tear-filled eyes. "Thank you."

Trevor chuckled. "You are the strangest woman. You'd have thought I gave you diamonds."

She hugged the little metal device to her chest. "This is better. It makes me feel better than any old diamond." Lana looked at the clothes she was wearing and at her purse. "Where should I put it? If I change clothes, it might get lost. If I put it in my purse, what are the chances my purse will remain with me?" Her brow furrowed. "My shoes?" She stared at her sneakers. "I wish I had a needle and thread. I could sew it into the side of my sneakers."

"We'll look for needle and thread in Bozeman."

"Thanks," Lana said and blinked back tears.

"Also…" He dug out his wallet and tried to hand it to her. "Take out a couple hundred dollars."

She frowned, refusing to handle the wallet. "Why?"

"You'll need it to buy clothes." He pushed it toward her. "Please, take it."

"I can't take your money. I have a credit card—" She stopped before she finished. "And it can be traced." Her lips twisted into a frown. She took the money out of his wallet. "I'll pay you back as soon as I can access my accounts."

"No hurry," he said. "Just be safe."

"I will." She shoved the bills into her purse and handed back his wallet. "Thanks again."

His heart was lighter than it had been in the past two years as he drove into Bozeman with the woman he loved at his side. A woman who got excited about a tracking device.

He hoped both trackers remained on her should anything happen to her.

Since he would be with her every second, he doubted they would need them. But the extra security made him feel better, just the same.

CHAPTER 12

LANA TUCKED the tracking device into the pocket of her jacket, telling herself she'd find some other way to carry it as she shopped for clothes to replace the ones in the trunk of the rental car.

And while they were at it, she wanted to buy a burner phone she could use if she needed to make a call. No one would associate the number with her. She'd be safe using it in the case of an emergency.

The need to remain incognito wasn't something she was used to. It took someone really special to be a spy. Lana wasn't feeling that special. She'd always been an open book to everyone she knew. She looked forward to the day she could get back to a normal life. Whatever that was. Since Mason's death, nothing had been normal. Not her, not the circumstances of his death and not the job she'd held at the DHS.

She wanted to call Peter and ask what was going

on with the director. Had the FBI caught up to him and arrested him? Lana shook her head. They wouldn't have been able to move that fast. Her data was a civilian's attempt at solving a crime. She didn't know squat about the legalities involved. The FBI would make sure they had all their ducks in a row before they went after the men plotting an attack on the government.

But would they be too late?

"Can we stop by Hank's place on the way back? I want to know if Swede was able to verify what I came up with and see if he found anything else that would help the FBI's case against the people involved."

"We can do that. If you don't mind, I'd like to grab lunch first. In fact, I'd like to get something to eat, now. I don't know about you, but breakfast seems like it was ages ago. And while you're shopping, find a pretty dress. I want to take you out on a real date."

Lana pressed a hand to her chest and gave him a fake surprised look, raised eyebrows and all. "Are you asking me out?" Her heart fluttered in her chest.

"Yes. I'm asking you out." He glanced her way. "You're okay with that, right?"

She laughed. "Yes, of course. Why wouldn't I be?"

Trevor sighed. "I'm still trying to find my way around the best buddy thing with Mason. In my heart, I know he'd be happy for us. But I still feel like I'm poaching on his territory."

Lana's gaze dropped to her lap, her joy at being asked on a date overshadowed by her loss and her feelings of guilt. "I have some of the same feelings. Like I'm not being true to my husband." She looked up. "Is it wrong to want to move on? I'm still alive. I can't stop living my life."

"No, you can't stop living. Had the roles been reversed, Mason would have grieved and moved on."

Lana nodded.

They chose to eat Italian. Soon after they completed their meal, Lana got serious about finding enough clothes to wear for a week. She started in lingerie because a lady couldn't go days without a change of panties. Especially if she had plans to be seen in said panties.

Her heartbeat quickened every time she thought about returning to the B&B and making love to Trevor in the white iron bed.

Panties and bras purchased, she moved on to find a second pair of blue jeans, a couple of shirts and finally the dress she'd wear on her first real date with Trevor.

"You're going to model them for me, aren't you?" he asked.

"No, I am not." She waved him away from the dressing rooms. "I want everything to be a surprise."

"You're no fun," he groused. "I'll be over here in the men's athletic shoes. Call me if you need someone to zip you."

He strolled away from the ladies' clothing into the men's shoe department. Within range she could call out if she needed anything.

With the help of one of the sales clerks, Lana gathered ten dresses and disappeared in the dressing room at the back of the store.

She tried on several black dresses that would do. Didn't every woman need a basic black dress she could dress up or down? But the red dress on the hanger in front of her called to her. She'd saved it for last. When she slipped it over her head and it glided down her body, she knew it was the one. It made her hair and eyes shine and fit her figure to perfection.

Determined to keep it completely secret from Trevor, she dressed in her old clothes, gathered her belongings and snuck out of the dressing room while Trevor's back was to her. She slipped through the clothing racks and found a register where she could pay for her purchases. The clerk wrapped the garments in a navy-blue plastic garment bag and tied it at the bottom.

Satisfied she'd gotten by without showing Trevor the dress, she grabbed the hanger and turned to find Peter Bishop, standing right behind her. Her heart thudded, and she glanced toward the back of the store for Trevor.

"Lana. Thank God, I found you."

Lana blinked. "Peter, what are you doing in Montana? How did you find me?"

"I had to come warn you. As soon as you left San Diego, I found out the Free America group has set a date. Their target date is tomorrow. They're going to execute their plan at ten o'clock tomorrow morning."

"Have you told the FBI?" Lana turned around, searching for Trevor. Oh, why had she snuck away? He needed to hear this. "Have you called the police? Notified the military?" Damn, Trevor was nowhere to be seen.

"No. I didn't think they'd believe me. You've already made an appointment with the FBI. They'll listen to you."

"How did find me?" She stood on her toes and peered over Peter's shoulder. "Where is he?"

"If you're looking for Anderson, he's waiting in the truck for you. I found him first. He said he had to get outside the store for his cellphone to work. He's in the truck." Peter gripped her arm and marched her toward the exit. "Come on. We have to let the right people know."

Unease prickled her skin. "Wait a minute." Lana dug her heels into the ground. "Trevor wouldn't have left the building without me."

"I told him I'd look out for you while he made a phone call to his boss, Hank Patterson." Peter gripped her elbow again and started for the exit. "We have no time to waste."

She tried to shake off his grip, but he held firm.

"I'm not going with you. How the hell did you find me, anyway? I didn't tell you where I was going."

"Yes, you did. When you called me at work, you told me you were heading to Montana."

Alarm bells rang in Lana's head. "No, I didn't." She reached into her purse for the stun gun Hank had loaned her. Peter's story wasn't right. He couldn't have known where she was going...unless he'd placed some kind of tracker on her or something she carried. "Let go of my arm, Peter."

His jaw tightened. "Lana, don't be difficult. You're the only other person who knows about what's going on. You have to come with me. Or else."

She refused to move from where she stood, her belly turning flips. Where was Trevor? "Or else what?"

Peter leaned close to her ear and whispered, "Or else, I hit the trigger to set off an explosion that will kill your boyfriend."

She stared hard at the man she'd thought was her friend. "What have you done to Trevor?"

"Nothing yet. But I just rigged an explosive in the dressing room you were using. The one you snuck out of. When he goes looking for you, he'll get more than he bargained for. Now, are you going to come with me?" He held up his free hand to show her small black device with a red button at the top. "Or do I press this? Are you going to cause a scene and force me to destroy your boyfriend?"

"You can't do that..." She frowned. "Can you?" She looked around at the other patrons of the store who could be injured in an explosion.

Where was Trevor?

"Time's up." He grabbed her arm again.

With her hand on the stun gun, she flipped the on switch. She let Peter guide her toward the front exit, all the while lifting her other hand out of the purse. She raised the stun gun but didn't get it to his body in time. He clamped a hand on her wrist and redirected the weapon, slamming it down on her thigh. The electrical charge hit her hard. Her knees buckled, and she dropped to the ground, the stun gun skittering across the smooth tile, out of reach.

The force of the shock left Lana stunned for several long seconds. Before she could gather her wits, Peter scooped her off the floor and hurried toward the door and out into the parking lot.

He stopped at a car illegally parked against the curb, leaned down and jerked the passenger door open, flung her into the seat and slammed shut the door. He slid across the hood of the vehicle, dropped down to the driver's side and jumped in.

By then, Lana had hold of the door handle and had pushed it open and prepared to jump out.

Peter lunged across the console, grabbed a handful of her hair and yanked her back inside. At the same time, he shifted into gear, hit the accelerator and shot the car forward.

Lana stared out at the parking lot. No one was within shouting distance. She couldn't believe this was happening to her. For the love of God, this was Montana! Where were all the cowboys when a woman needed one?

Peter was out of the parking lot and onto the street in seconds, headed out of Bozeman onto the highway.

If Lana tried to throw herself out of the moving vehicle, she'd likely break every bone in her body as well as peel away layers of skin with road burn. Her best option was to wait for the man to slow to a stop. Then she could punch him in the throat, leap out of the vehicle and run for her life.

Outside town, she thought she might get that chance.

Peter pulled to the side of the road.

Lana flung open the car door and rolled out onto the ground, gathered her feet beneath her and took off.

She hadn't gone ten yards when she was hit in the backs of her knees in a flying tackle. She landed on her chest, the air knocked from her lungs and a heavy weight lying across her legs and back.

"Damned woman. I should have killed you back in San Diego." Peter jerked her arms behind her back and wrapped duct tape around her wrists.

When he stood, he jerked her onto her feet.

Lana bent over and plowed into the man's belly, hitting him hard with her head.

He stumbled backward, regained his balance and was ready when she tried the same trick again. This time, he backhanded her so hard, she saw stars and the world spun. She had to get away. Peter had been the man who'd attacked her back in San Diego. He was the one who'd tried to kill her three times already. If she didn't get away, this time, he'd succeed.

He hit her again, and the world went black.

CHAPTER 13

Trevor had been standing near the dressing room doors when a young mother came up to him, frantic and in tears.

"Please help me. I can't find my son," she twisted her hands together, and her bottom lip trembled. "He's only three. Oh, sweet Lord. I let go of him for only a couple seconds...and he disappeared. Please, please, help me find him."

Trevor shot a glance toward the changing rooms, and then back to the woman. "Let's go to one of the clerks, she can send out a call over the intercom to help you look for your son. What is his name?"

"His name is Dalton. Please, I have to find him. He's my baby. He doesn't know any better. He'll be so scared. And God forbid he wanders out of the store and into the street. Sweet Jesus, help me."

With the woman sobbing noisily, Trevor marched

her over to one of the registers. He couldn't see the changing rooms, but he figured he wouldn't be away for any more than a minute or two.

The register he took the woman to was closed, and he ended up taking her to another even farther away from the dressing room.

By that time, a clerk was found leading a little boy by the hand. The child had tears streaming down his cheeks. When he saw his mother, he flung himself into her arms and cried along with his distraught mother.

Trevor turned to leave, but the mother caught his arm and engulfed him in a soggy hug, thanking him profusely for helping her find her son.

He finally had to untangle the woman's arms from around his neck and beat a hasty retreat before she tried again to thank him.

Trevor hurried back to the dressing room in the ladies' department. When he reached it, he couldn't hear anyone moving around inside. He tried to capture the attention of one of the clerks, but there didn't appear to be anyone working the area. He gave up and entered the dressing room, checking behind each door, calling out, "Lana!" Even before he neared the last door, he knew. She wasn't there.

Still not too concerned, he emerged and glanced around at the racks of women's clothing. Across the room he spied a woman about Lana's height and build with sandy-blond hair rifling through dresses.

Trevor wove his way through the racks and placed his hand on her shoulder. "You nearly scared the life out of me."

The woman turned, her eyes wide. "Excuse me?" She wasn't Lana.

"My apologies. I thought you were someone else." Trevor backed away and spent the next few minutes searching through the vast displays of women's clothing, searching for one woman. He returned to the dressing rooms and called out her name. "Lana!"

A clerk stepped out of one of the rooms carrying several dresses. "Are you looking for the blonde who was here a few minutes ago?"

"Yes, ma'am."

"It's really strange. She paid for her purchases, but then she dropped them on her way out." The woman walked toward the register and lifted a navy-blue plastic wrapped bag. "If you know her, could you see that she gets her clothes. I'm sure she'll realize she left this as soon as she gets home."

Trevor's pulse thundered in his ears, and his fists clenched. "Did you actually see her leave?"

She shook her head. "A man she seemed to know came up to her as she finished paying for her items. I had to go assist another customer and didn't see her leave." The clerk frowned. "Do you think she's all right? Should I call for the police?"

"Do me a favor and get on your intercom. Page Lana Connolly."

The woman nodded and lifted the microphone. She did as Trevor suggested and asked for Lana Connolly to report to the register near the dressing rooms.

Trevor waited a minute, then another, but Lana didn't appear. "Call the police, the national guard, the Navy SEALs and I don't care who else. I think she's been kidnapped."

Trevor started for the door at a run. His foot kicked something pink, sending it shooting out in front of him. He would have ignored it, but it caught his eye. When he bent to pick it up, his heart sank even deeper into his gut. It was Lana's stun gun.

He pulled his cell phone from his pocket and called Hank. "I need as many of the Brotherhood as you can gather and turn on the trackers. Someone snatched Lana."

THE POUNDING in her head woke Lana. When she blinked open her eyes, she still couldn't see. Everything was black. As her vision and her mind cleared, she felt around her. She lay on what she could swear was a felt-lined floor. When she raised her hands, they bumped into something metal. Then an engine revved to life, and her tomb moved. That's when she realized she was in the trunk of a vehicle.

She banged her forehead against the trunk lid and

yelled. "Help! I'm in here! Help! I'm being kidnapped! Please. Help me!"

No one came to her rescue, and the vehicle increased its speed.

For a long time, Lana worked at the inside of the trunk. She found a metal edge and sawed her wrists across it until the duct tape broke, and she was able to free her hands. Running her fingers around the interior, she searched for a way to release the trunk lid, but to no avail. If she could push through the back seat into the passenger area of the car, she might be able to overpower her abductor and escape.

She rubbed her fingers raw, scratching at the felt, pushing at the back of the seat and scouring every corner, looking for a lever or anything that would lay the seat down and allow her to climb through, but only managed to break nails. She was trapped.

The vehicle kept a fast, steady pace, indicating they were on a highway. Occasionally the driver slowed for curves, but he didn't stop again.

The constant rumble of the road eventually lulled Lana back to sleep. She didn't wake again until the vehicle came to a full stop, and the engine was turned off.

Lana couldn't tell how long she'd been asleep or how long they'd been on the road. For all she knew, they could be anywhere, and Trevor wouldn't know where to look.

Then she remembered the tracking device she'd

stuffed into the pocket of her jacket. She ran her hands along her sides before she remembered she'd shed her jacket when she'd been trying on clothes. She must have dropped it when Peter had attacked her.

Her heart sank. Without the tracking device, Trevor wouldn't know where to look for her. She couldn't count on the cavalry coming to the rescue. This was a situation she'd have to deal with on her own.

Footsteps sounded outside the vehicle. The crunching sound indicated gravel.

Lana bunched her muscles, ready to spring out of the trunk as soon as Peter opened the lid.

Men spoke in low tones, their words muffled by the walls of the trunk.

Lana's hopes dipped even more. Defending herself against one man was difficult enough. Two men could easily overpower her.

She stiffened her spine. Whatever happened, she wouldn't go down without a fight. If she could surprise them and hit them hard, she might buy herself enough time to run for the woods.

The metal click of the trunk lock releasing warned her to be ready. She closed her eyes and pretended she was still unconscious. Since light didn't push through her eyelids, she assumed it was night. Good. If she got a running start, she could hide in the dark.

"What do you want me to do with her?" Peter said as he opened the trunk.

"Why did you bring her here in the first place?"

"I figured it would be easier to hide the body in the backwoods here than on the highway getting here."

"Idiot," the other man cursed. "With the FBI alerted to our efforts, we can't stay here. You should have dealt with her before she made her appointment with the FBI."

"Believe me, I tried. I wasn't counting on an ex-Navy SEAL showing up."

"You should have killed him, too."

"Again, I tried," Peter said.

Lana's fists bunched. The bastard deserved to die, and she hoped she could help in that regard.

"Well, your incompetence is costing us big. Now, we're having to move up our deadline, take on a lesser target and expose our purpose before we can mobilize the other components of our organization across the country."

"Again, what do you want me to do with her now?"

"We don't have time to deal with a body, and if we're here for long, it'll begin to smell. Put her with the other detainees. When we leave, we'll torch the place with them inside."

Lana fought to keep from jumping out of the trunk and punching the other speaker in the throat.

How could anyone talk so callously about burning people alive?

"Let's get her out. We have a lot to do to prepare for tomorrow."

Hands grabbed her arms and pulled her up over the edge of the trunk. More hands gripped her ankles.

As soon as she was completely out of the trunk, Lana twisted violently.

The men holding her lost their grips and dropped her to the ground.

She immediately rolled away from them, lurched to her feet and ran.

Lana made it to the edge of a clearing when she was hit from behind. She went down cursing and kicking at the hands grabbing for her ankles. No sooner had she freed herself from their grip and scrambled to her feet, then another set of hands gripped her arm and twisted it up behind her back, pushing it high between her shoulder blades.

Pain ripped through her shoulder, forcing her up on her toes to relieve the pressure.

"Secure her wrists. We can't have her running off to warn more authorities. She's done enough damage."

Peter came at her with a roll of duct tape and wrapped it around her ankles while the other man held her. Then he bound her wrists.

"I've got her," Peter said and tossed Lana over

his shoulder in a fireman's carry. He walked through what appeared to be a make-shift camp, populated with a couple shacks and green military-issue tents.

"Peter, what are you doing? Why are you with these people?" Lana spoke quietly between having her diaphragm gouged by his shoulder as he walked across the rough terrain.

"Shut up."

"But you're not one of these fanatics. You care about our country."

"You don't know anything. You started this investigation knowing nothing about what you were digging into. I should never have gotten involved, but I did. Now, it's too late."

"No, Peter. It's not too late. You can get out of this. All you have to do is walk away," she insisted. He might be her only hope for getting out of the mess she found herself in.

"I said, shut up," he bit out. "Once you're in, you don't get out. Alive."

Lana could sense the fear in his voice. "What happened?" she asked. "How did you get this deep?"

"The director caught me looking into the files. He gave me two choices, join them or find myself at the bottom of the bay wearing cement overshoes. I chose to live."

"And to kill for them?"

"It was kill you or be killed. I like living, so it was

you that had to go." He slowed, hefted her up on his shoulder and continued moving.

"Where is the director now, Peter?"

"He's here. When he found out you were going to the FBI, he left San Diego and came here. You have no idea how influential the man is. If I'd known, I wouldn't have offered to help you. I wouldn't be here now."

"Peter, you can't let them push you into something you'll regret."

"I already regret getting involved with you. But there's nothing I can do to stop what's about to happen. So, stop talking before you get me in more trouble than I already am."

"Peter, they're going to kill me."

"Good. If I'd done it right, you'd already be dead, and the mission wouldn't have been compromised. You've pissed off a lot of people."

Men stood in groups, their dark silhouettes standing still as Peter passed them and entered one of the shacks made of plywood and tin.

The shack was divided into two rooms. The front room appeared to be an office of sorts with maps tacked to the walls along with signs stating things like, *Take Back America, Politicians Must Die* and *Our Government Sucks!*

A door at the far end of the room had a bar across it, locking it from the outside.

A large man with a grizzled beard pulled the lever

up and opened the door. He shined a flashlight into the room. "Try anything, and I'll feed you to the bears in pieces tonight."

Whimpers sounded from inside the dark room.

Peter dumped Lana in the middle of the dirt floor and backed out of the room.

Lana tried one last time. "Peter, don't do this. You're not one of them."

"Shut up, bitch!" he said and slammed the door.

Lana lay in the dark. Before the door had been shut, she'd noticed several other people inside. All women, their faces drawn, tear-streaked and terrified.

"Will someone help me get out of this duct tape?" she asked.

When no one moved, she added, "Please."

"If we help you, they'll beat us," a women's whisper sounded in the darkness.

"They beat us when we talk to each other," another said. "Don't talk."

"Help me, and I won't have to talk," Lana said.

Pounding thundered against the wall. "Shut the fuck up in there!"

The shuffle of movement sounded beside Lana, and fingers felt along her arm from her shoulder to where the tape bound her wrists. After much tugging and picking, the fingers pulled the tape free a little at a time, easing it loose to keep from making any loud noises.

Lana bit down on her bottom lip to keep from crying out as the last layer pulled free of her wrists, seemingly taking a layer of skin with it.

"Thank you," she said softly. Once her hands were freed, she pulled her knees up to her chin and went to work on the tape around her ankles. Little by little, she eased the tape loose and set it aside. She might be able to use it in some capacity. "Is there any way out of this cell?" she asked so softly, only those who were in the room could have heard her.

"No," one woman answered.

She scuffed her shoe against the hard-packed floor. "The floor is dirt, have you tried digging your way out?"

"We have no tools," someone said.

"What about the roof?" Lana ran her fingers along the wall, reaching as high as she could. The shack wasn't all that tall. She could feel where the metal roof connected with the walls. "Can one of you give me a boost so I can check it out?"

"Please, don't. Ray will hear you."

Lana assumed Ray was the hulking jerk who'd opened the door for Peter.

"He'll come in and beat you with a metal rod," another woman said.

A sob sounded from the corner. "He broke my arm."

Lana's heart contracted, and her back stiffened. These women had been abused. She had to get them out before they were burned to death. "Look, they plan on burning this place to the ground, with us in it. If you want to live, you'll help me."

Silence greeted her whispered entreaty.

A moment later, a hand reached out to touch her arm. "I'll bend down. You can step on my back," a young voice said.

"What's your name?" Lana asked.

"Rebecca."

"Thank you, Rebecca." Lana waited for the woman to hunker down. Then she gently stepped onto her back and pushed her hand against the corrugated tin roof.

The sheet held fast.

"We need to move over and try again." Lana climbed down. "Move to your right."

Rebecca crawled to her right. "Go ahead."

Lana stepped up onto her back and pushed her hands against the tin. The panel moved. Lana pushed a little harder. This time, the panel raised up several inches. "It's loose," she whispered. She raised it up and ran her hand over the top of the wall and felt a cool breeze caress her skin.

She jumped down and helped her new friend to her feet. "We need something to prop the roof panel up, so we can slip over the edge. Is there anything in here? A bench, chair, stool, piece of wood. Anything?"

"Nothing," Rebecca responded. "They cleared the room completely before putting us in here."

"Why are you segregated from the others?" Lana asked.

"For different reasons," Rebecca answered. "I refused to have sex with my husband until I was past my monthly cycle."

"Oh, dear Lord," Lana hugged Rebecca. "Does he know Ray is beating you?"

"He doesn't care. But I fear for my children. He has no patience with them."

"What about the rest of you?"

"I burned supper two nights in a row," another woman said. "My daughter has been sick, and I neglected the food on the fire to take care of her."

"I disagreed with my husband in front of others," a woman said softly. "I knew I shouldn't, but it just came out."

Each woman had a story that broke Lana's heart. "Why do you stay with these men?" she asked.

"We have children and no money. How would we provide for them?"

"There are services that would help you until you could get back on your feet. You don't have to put up with this abuse."

"They'll steal our children from us," Rebecca said. "We can't abandon our children."

"You don't understand," Lana said. "They plan on leaving this camp and burning this building to the ground. *With. You. In. It.*" She paused for emphasis. "If you want to live to help your children, we need get the hell out of here."

"You can use my shoe to hold the roof up," one of the women whispered.

"Honey, it'll take more than one shoe to hold it high enough."

Eight shoes were shoved into her hands.

"This might work." For the first time since she was captured, hope surged.

Lana added her shoes to the pile and, with the help of her new friends, she stacked them in between the ceiling and the wall to prop up the corrugated tin roof panel high enough to allow a person to squeeze through the gap.

Outside the shack, the camp had come alive with men moving about, shouting orders. Someone had fired up a generator to power lights. The gap in the ceiling allowed a little of that light to penetrate their little cell.

Lana could finally see the women she shared the small space with. They each had circles beneath their eyes, bruises on their arms and faces and dirty, bedraggled hair and clothing.

When she got them out of there, she'd make certain they and their children found a safe, clean place to go to. But first, they had to get out of the building the men were planning to raze.

CHAPTER 14

WITHIN FORTY-FIVE MINUTES of Trevor's call, Hank arrived in Bozeman with five of his men from the Brotherhood Protectors.

Navy SEALs Swede, Chuck Johnson, Caleb "Maddog" Maddox and Brandon "Boomer" Rayne. Army Ranger Alex "Taz" Davila, Delta Force dog handler Joseph "Kujo" Kuntz and his dog Six rounded out the team of seven highly trained, former special operations fighters.

Swede brought with him a handheld tracking monitor and was already following Lana's progress. "They're headed into the Bitterroot Mountains." He looked up from the display. "That's not all. I got word from the FBI that they received an anonymous tip from a guy identifying himself as WolfST6. He said the Free America group has started a countdown. The time ends tomorrow at eleven hundred hours. He deciphered an encrypted message from the group with what he presumes are a grid coordinates."

"Did you plot the coordinates on a map?"

"We did," Hank said. "And we looked for what events are taking place at the location tomorrow at that time. The president of the United States is scheduled to give a speech at Montana's state capitol building in Helena tomorrow at that exact time."

"They're going to attack the president," Trevor said. "Frankly, I don't give a rat's ass about what happens to the president. He has an entire team of Secret Service bodyguards protecting him. Lana has no one. Where is she now?" He leaned over the display in Swede's hand.

"Near the foothills of the Bitterroot Mountains." Swede pointed to the map on the display screen. They have an hour's head start on us."

"Then we have no time to lose." Trevor jerked his head toward his truck. "Swede, you're riding with me."

Hank tossed his truck keys to Chuck. "Anderson's truck will take the lead. You guys follow. Those of you along for the ride can prep the weapons and make sure they're primed and ready to deploy."

"Yes, sir," Chuck said. He slid behind the steering wheel.

"I call shotgun." Maddog climbed into the passenger seat.

Taz and Kujo slipped into the backseat with Kujo's dog Six in the middle.

"Do you want to drive?" Trevor said to Hank, even as he climbed into the driver's seat.

"No. You can take the wheel. Swede, we need you up front with that monitor." Hank slipped into the back seat with a duffle bag full of weapons and ammunition.

"She's an hour ahead of us. One of the tracking devices is in this truck, but the other one's still moving. I would assume it's Lana." Trevor stared down at the monitor as he started the truck engine. "Hold on to your bootstraps, we're going to be flying." He slammed his foot against the accelerator and shot out of town on the main road leading across the state and into the mountains. With Lana an hour ahead of them, they had to make up the time somehow.

He kicked up his speed to over ninety-five miles per hour, praying a state policeman didn't pull him over and slow him down.

By the time they reached the foothills of the Bitterroot Mountains, the sun had edged down below the tallest peaks, casting long shadows over the valleys. They'd been forced to slow considerably as the roads curved and twisted through the hills and mountains.

All the while, Swede fed Trevor directions. So far, the little green dot on the screen was moving. Where it stopped would be where they found Lana. Hopefully, alive.

Darkness settled over the land when Swede finally announced, "They've stopped."

Trevor slowed long enough to look down at where Swede pointed at the map on the monitor. "It appears they're out in the middle of nowhere. I don't see any roads where they are."

"How far out are we?"

"I'd guess we have another thirty minutes until we arrive," Swede said.

"You made good time, speeding through the flatlands." Hank leaned between the seats and stared at the screen. "You had me worried a couple of times, taking the curves a little faster than I would have."

Trevor glanced in the rearview mirror. The trailing vehicle had kept up with them all the way.

"You know the drill," Hank said.

Trevor nodded. "We stop somewhere between one or two miles short of our destination and hike in on foot."

The rest of the journey was conducted in silence, the tension rising as the Trevor closed the distance between the team of Brotherhood Protectors and Lana's tracking device. He prayed she still wore the necklace, and that they weren't chasing a false lead into the mountains.

Twenty-five minutes later, Swede looked up. "You

should look for a place to pull off the road. We're getting close."

Trevor found a dirt road leading off the highway. It appeared to have been used recently, with fresh, wet potholes and deep-rutted tire tracks.

He bumped off the road and into the woods, bringing the truck to a stop behind a stand of trees and bushes. As soon as he shifted into park, he dropped down from the truck and waited impatiently for Swede to disembark.

Swede glanced at the device, and then raised a finger to point. "She's approximately one and a half miles in that direction." The route was packed with trees and underbrush, and it rose up a steady incline. The going would be rough.

"Let's get a move on."

The team met between the two vehicles and took quick stock of the firepower Hank had brought along. They adjusted radio headsets in their ears and tested them to make sure they worked.

Trevor grabbed an AR 15 rifle with a powerful scope. With the rifle, the handgun he had tucked beneath his jacket, his Ka-Bar knife and several magazines filled with ammunition, he was more than ready to rescue Lana. Trevor fell in beside Swede as they moved toward their goal.

The team fanned out, moving through the woods, down into ravines and up sharp ridges.

On point with Swede, Trevor emerged at the top

of a hill overlooking what appeared to be a camp in the middle of a small valley. Vehicle headlights shone brightly, and shadowy figures appeared to be loading things into the trucks.

"She's down there," Swede said.

Hank stood on the other side of Swede and spoke into his headset. "Come up to the ridgeline," he ordered the others.

One by one, the team reported in.

Hank studied the camp below through binoculars. "I see men moving about. But I don't see any women or children." He handed the binoculars to Trevor.

Trevor adjusted the settings and stared down at the camp. As Hank had indicated, the camp seemed to be in a flurry of activity, loading vehicles with boxes. At the far-left end of the valley was what looked like an old school bus. Movement beside the bus caught his attention. "The women and children are being loaded into an old school bus. They appear to be carrying bags and suitcases."

"They're bugging out," Swede said. He lowered his binoculars and studied the monitor's screen. "Ms. Connolly isn't in that group. She's near the back of the camp, but in the middle. There appears to be a hut of some sort there."

"I'm going down." Trevor slipped over the crown of the ridge.

"Not without us," Hank said.

"If you're coming, let's get a move on."

"What the hell are they doing?" Swede said. He was still looking through the binoculars at the camp below. "Damn."

"What?" Trevor raised field glasses to his eyes and took a moment to focus on the valley below.

Several men carried what appeared to be jugs, and they were shaking them around the outsides of the only two permanent structures on the camp—one of which Lana's tracking device indicated she was inside.

"They're spreading accelerant around the buildings. We have to get down there. Now."

His rifle in hand, Trevor raced down the hill, not giving a damn that he was making enough noise to wake the dead.

The bastards were lighting the buildings on fire.

With Lana inside.

CHAPTER 15

THE SHOUTING CONTINUED OUTSIDE the building, and then it got quiet.

Lana turned to Rebecca. "Boost me up."

Rebecca cupped her hands.

Lana stepped one foot into them and pulled herself up to the ledge to look outside.

A man ran along the outside of the building, shaking a large jug.

"Hurry!" someone called out to him. "Or they'll leave without us."

The man flung the jug at the building. It bounced off the plywood siding, sloshing liquid on the ground.

An acrid scent rose in the air, stinging Lana's nostrils.

Then the man lit a match and tossed it at the jug.

Lana watched in horror as the flame flew through the night. When the flame snuffed out before it hit the ground, Lana let out the breath she'd been holding.

But another match followed the first. This time the flame hit the liquid, and it caught, traveling over the ground toward the wall of the hut.

Lana tried to keep from panicking. The last thing she needed was to trigger pandemonium among the prisoners in the hut. She waited until the man rounded the corner of the hut, and then pulled herself up to the top of the wall, pushing the tin roof of the building up with her shoulder. "Time to go, ladies," she called down to the group below. "Don't hesitate. We only have minutes to spare."

Rebecca and Mary Beth helped shove the others up the wall, one by one. Lana straddled the wall and pulled with all her might to get each one up to the top and over.

Each time, the ladies balked at dropping down into the gasoline-fed flames.

Lana assured them they had no other choice. "Drop and roll," she instructed each. "Now, go!" If the woman didn't go immediately, she gave her a shove. She didn't have time to be nice. Not if she wanted to get all the women out before the building burned to the ground.

The last one in the building was Rebecca.

Lana held out her hand. "Take my hand. I'll pull you up." Flames licked at her feet. They had seconds before the flames consumed the hut.

"I'm not going," Rebecca backed away.

Lana stared down at the woman, her heart breaking at the desperation on Rebecca's face.

"If I live, he'll find me. He'll make me come back to him."

Lana held out her hand. "You have to live to get your children back. They deserve a better life than what your husband will give them."

"I'm tired. I can't do this anymore."

Smoke filtered into the building as flames ate through the other side.

Rebecca coughed and covered her mouth.

"If you don't come up here, I'll be forced to come down and get you. I'm not leaving here without you." Lana swung her leg over the side, back into the hut.

"No." Rebecca raised her hand. "You can't sacrifice yourself for me. I'm not worthy."

"Bullshit. You're worth more than that sack-of-shit husband of yours, who left you to die. Get your ass up here now, or I'm coming down after you." The smoke stung Lana's eyes and threatened to choke her. She coughed and pulled her shirt up over her nose.

Still, Rebecca hesitated.

"Coming down," Lana said.

"No. I'm coming up," Rebecca held out her hand.

Lana shifted her leg to the other side of the wall, grabbed Rebecca's hand and pulled as hard as she could.

Rebecca clasped her hand and tried to swing her leg up to the wall's ledge but missed. She fell, losing her grip and dropped to the ground.

"Go," she said. "Save yourself."

"I told you, I'm not going without you." Lana dropped to the ground beside Rebecca. "Get up there." She cupped her hands. "Now!"

Rebecca placed her foot in Lana's hands and pulled herself up onto the ledge. "But now you can't get out."

"I'll get out. Go on. Help the others hide in the woods."

"But—"

"Go!" Lana said and coughed. "Just go!"

Tears streamed down Rebecca's cheeks.

Lana pushed at her leg. "Please. I'll get out of this. I promise."

The next moment, Rebecca slipped over the ledge and dropped out of sight.

Alone in the hut, fire burning all around, her eyes stinging so badly she could hardly see, Lana wondered if she'd be able to live up to her promise. If she would live.

Her lungs burned, and she struggled to breathe the smoke-laden air. She couldn't give up. Trevor was out there somewhere. Her chance at a happy-ever-after life would not slip through her fingers this time, damn it!

She ran toward the wall and threw herself at it with all the determination of a climber on Mt Everest.

THE BUSLOAD of women and children left the compound before the Trevor and his team reached the outer perimeter.

The men were piling into trucks rumbling toward the road leading out.

Hank, Taz, Kujo, Chuck and Boomer set out to head off the trucks attempting to leave.

Swede stayed with Trevor as they raced for the burning building where Lana's beacon still blinked green on the tracker screen.

The hut was fully engulfed in flames. That didn't stop Trevor. He ran for the door and flung it open.

The heat burst from inside, nearly knocking him down. Trevor pulled his shirt up to cover his face, ducked low and ran into the flames. Smoke hit his eyes, making him blink. The room was empty, but there was a door with a heavy wooden bar locked in place.

Rage burned hotter than the inferno around him. Bastards! Trevor ran for the door, pushed the bar up and ripped it open.

At that moment, the wall on one side of the hut buckled. Trevor knew he had to get out, but not without Lana.

The inner room was filled with smoke.

"Lana!" he called out, inhaled a lungful of smoke and coughed. He dropped to his hands and knees and looked around at the floor. No one was in the room.

Still on his hands and knees, he crawled through the smoke and fire out into the night air.

Swede stood with his arm around a woman's waist, his other hand holding his rifle. "Damn it, Anderson. That has to be the stupidest thing you've ever done."

"She..." he coughed, "wasn't...in...there."

"Oh, thank God." The woman in Swede's arm dropped to her knees. "She told me to get the women into the woods. I did, and I came back for her." She sobbed into her hands. "She got out. Sweet heaven, she got out."

Gunfire sounded behind them where the rest of the team dealt with the men leaving the camp in the loaded trucks.

Trevor lurched to his feet. "If she got out, where is she? Lana!" he yelled.

"Looking for her?" a male voice called out. A tall man wearing a leather bomber jacket and carrying a submachine gun stepped into the open, holding Lana by her hair.

Joy rushed through Trevor. In the light from the

flames, he could see the soot smeared across Lana's face. Her eyes were red-rimmed, and her clothes were black with dirt and soot. But she was alive.

His joy faded as he noted the submachinegun pressed to Lana's temple.

Anger sent a wash of red across Trevor's vision. How dare this man threaten Lana's life? She was a good person and deserved to be treated better than this. He clenched his fists, ready to charge the man and beat the living shit out of him.

"Trevor, don't worry about me. I've got this," Lana assured him.

She was trying to make him okay with the fact she could be murdered in front of him? Trust her to worry more about others than herself. This was the woman meant for him.

Trevor wasn't going to let this lunatic ruin his second chance with the woman he loved.

"Drop your weapons," the man said, "and maybe I'll let her live."

"Don't do it," Lana said. "This sorry ass is Huntley Powell, my boss at the Department of Homeland Security. He's a traitor to our country, and he doesn't deserve to live."

"Shut the hell up," he said and yanked her hair so hard, she stumbled backward. "I should have killed you myself. That bumbling idiot botched all of this, letting you get to the FBI before we had a chance to carry through on our plan. I should have killed him sooner."

"Sooner?" Lana shot a glance toward Powell. "What did you do to Peter?"

"What I should have done as soon as he failed to take care of you."

"You killed him?" Her teeth bared in a snarl. "He might have been salvageable, unlike you." She crossed her arms over her chest and glared at the man holding the machinegun to her temple. "What gives you the right to take the lives of other human beings?"

He snorted and tapped her temple with the muzzle of the machinegun. "This gives me the right. This country has gone to shit. The politicians are making a shambles of our government and our standing among foreign nations. It's time someone took control and stopped the absurdity."

"Well, someone needs to stop you." Lana ducked quickly, drove her elbow into Powell's gut and dove behind him.

Powell swung his weapon toward Trevor and Swede.

Trevor took the only chance he had and fired on Powell before he could fire on them. He hit him with his first shot.

The man stood as if he hadn't been hit full-on in the chest. He raised his weapon and stared directly at Trevor.

Trevor and Swede dropped to the ground as a burst of bullets ripped through the air over their heads.

Then Powell crumpled to the ground like a rag doll, the machinegun slipping free of his grip.

Lana grabbed for the weapon and stood over the man, her eyes wide and angry. She pulled the trigger, but the weapon jammed. She pulled back the bolt and let it slam forward and tried to pull the trigger again, and it jammed again. "Dammit!"

Swede laughed. "Remind me not to piss off your girlfriend. I'm going to go see if I can help the others, now that you have this situation in hand." Swede left Trevor and ran toward the trucks stalled at the exit at the compound.

Trevor crossed to Lana, removed the machinegun from her grip and threw it to the side. Then he pulled her into his arms and held her shaking body.

"These men should die," Lana sobbed into his shirt. "They abuse women, frighten children and kill good people." Her fingers curled into his shirt, and she looked up into his eyes, tears making dark streaks down her face. "You found me. How?"

He touched the necklace around her throat. "I didn't want to lose you ever again. I put a tracking device on you."

"But I put it in my jacket pocket. The jacket I left at the store back in Bozeman."

He smiled and kissed the tip of her soot-smudged nose. "I gave you two. One of them is in the necklace you're wearing."

She wrapped her arms around his waist and hugged him tight. "I didn't think you'd find me. I was going to get myself out of this situation if it was the last thing I did."

And it had almost been the last thing she'd done. Trevor swallowed hard on the lump forming in his throat. "Lana, sweetheart, I need to tell you something before anything else happens to you."

She looked up at him, a frown denting her brow. "What is it?" Her frown deepened as she looked into his face. "What's wrong?" She leaned back and ran her gaze over his body. "Were you hurt?"

He chuckled. "I'm fine, but I don't think my heart will ever be quite the same."

She leaned her ear against his chest. "It sounds fine to me."

He gripped her face and forced her to look him in the eyes. "Woman, will you just listen to what I have to say?"

She nodded. "Shoot."

"I love you, Lana." He kissed her forehead. "I've loved you for a very long time. Even before Mason beat me to popping the question, I've loved you." He dug in his pocket and pulled out a small box, now covered in soot. "I bought this before he asked you to marry him. I was waiting for the perfect moment to ask you. But I waited too long. Mason got there first." He dropped to one knee next to the dead director, a burning building puffing smoke into the air and did what he should have done two years ago.

"Lana, will you give me that second chance I don't deserve, and do me the honor of being my wife? I promise to love, honor and cherish you for the rest of my life. And at this rate, that might not be too long. Please, say yes before anything else happens."

The roof of the hut crashed to the ground behind them, sending out a shower of sparks.

Tears spilled from Lana's eyes, and she dropped to her knees in front of him. "Are you sure? Do you really want to marry this mess of a woman? Knowing I was married to your best friend?"

"Mason would have wanted us to be together. I think he knew how much I loved you. But he loved you, too. I don't blame him for holding onto you with both hands. He was faster and smarter than I was. But this old dog can learn from his mistakes."

Lana pressed a finger to Trevor's lips. "Yes."

"I promise you I'll take care of you. I'll give you all the children you want and even change diapers."

She shook her head, smiling, her teeth white in the darkness of her dirty face. "I said yes."

Trevor shut up and let her words sink in. She'd said yes. His heart filled to overflowing, threatening to burst right out of his chest. He rose to his feet, bringing her with him. Then he took the ring he'd purchased two years ago out of the box and slipped it onto her finger where it had always belonged. "I love you, Lana. Always have. Always will."

EPILOGUE

"Need another lemonade?"

Lana tipped back her head and smiled at Trevor. "Not yet. I haven't finished the one I have. But thanks." She sat back in the lounge chair on Hank and Sadie's wide porch, happier than she'd been in a very long time.

"The bridesmaids dresses are supposed to come in this week," Sadie said.

"The florist said she can get the white daisies you requested for your bouquet." Boomer's wife, Daphne, dropped down on the seat beside Lana. "All we need is a band, and we'll be set for next month."

Lana smiled. "Now that the ladies and the children from the Free America compound are settled in their temporary lodging at Mrs. Kinner's B&B, I feel like I can think about the wedding."

"I hope they keep their husbands in jail for a very

long time," Molly, Kujo's girl, said. "I couldn't get over the number of bruises those women had all over their bodies. Those men should never be free."

"Agreed. Sadie and Hank were kind enough to rent out the B&B for a year, so they could get situated and have a place to stay until they get on their feet, find jobs and can support their children on their own." Lana drew in a deep breath and let it out. "Which brings us back to the subject of the wedding. Do you think we can move up the date?"

"What?" Trevor straightened from his position leaning against the porch railing. "You want to get married sooner? I thought all brides needed time to plan everything."

Lana frowned, though the corners of her lips twitched. "You're not getting cold feet, are you?"

He reached for her hands and pulled her to her feet. "No way. I'd marry you tonight if we could nab a preacher."

"Good," Lana brushed a kiss across his lips. "But a week from now will be soon enough."

"A week?" Sadie and Daphne squeaked at once. "We can't possibly get everything ready in a week."

"Then we won't worry about the things that we can't do," Lana said. "I'd like to be married as soon as possible, so I can go on my honeymoon before I'm too big to enjoy it with my man."

"What? You...too big?" Trevor shook his head. "You eat like a bird. That'll never happen."

"Sweetheart, it's about to get real," she said and shifted his hand from her arm to her belly. She reached into her pocket and pulled out a plastic wand. "The blue line means positive."

Trevor shook his head again. "Positive for what?"

Sadie and Daphne both dissolved into laughter.

"What's so funny?" Hank climbed the steps to the porch, smiling.

Swede, Boomer, Kujo and Chuck all gathered around.

"Yeah, let us in on the joke," Chuck said, holding Daphne's baby girl, Maya.

"Lana's pregnant," Sadie announced.

"And the wedding date just got moved up." Daphne clapped her hands. "We're having a wedding next week."

Trevor's eyes widened. "A baby? You're pregnant with a baby?" He ran his hand over her flat belly. "Are you sure?"

She nodded. "It moves our plans forward a little, but the house should be finished before the baby arrives, and we'll have time to get furniture for the nursery." Lana stared up into Trevor's eyes. "You are happy, aren't you?"

He nodded. "I've never been happier in my life." Then he grabbed her around the waist and swung her around. "I'm going to be a daddy!"

When he set her back on her feet, he kissed her soundly. "Let's have a wedding."

She laughed, her heart swelling in her chest. "Trevor?"

"Yes, darlin'," he said.

"If this baby is a boy…could we call him Mason?"

Trevor swallowed hard, and his eyes glittered with moisture. "I wouldn't call him anything else. Mason was just as much a part of my life as you are." He led Lana over to the porch swing and settled her in beside him. "If it's a girl, we can call her Maisie. The main thing is that this child will know how much I love you and how much I love him."

"Or her." Lana leaned into Trevor, her love for the man filling her life so completely.

In her heart she knew Mason would have approved and would have been happy that she'd gotten on with her life and found someone who loved her as much as he had. "I love you, Trevor. Forever and always."

THE END

THANK you for reading Montana SEAL Friendly Fire. The Brotherhood Protectors Series continues with Montana SEAL's Mail-Order Bride. Keep reading for the 1st Chapter.

. . .

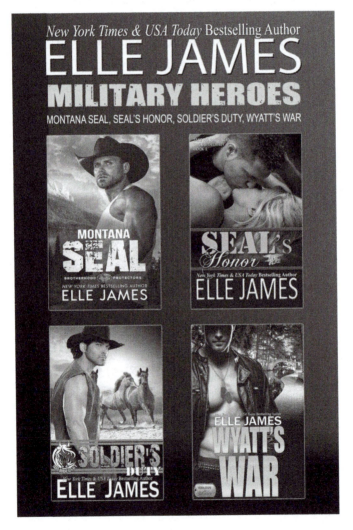

Visit ellejames.com for more titles and release dates
For hot cowboys, visit her alter ego Myla Jackson at
mylajackson.com
and join Elle James and Myla Jackson's Newsletter at
http://ellejames.com/ElleContact.htm

MONTANA SEAL'S MAIL-ORDER BRIDE

BROTHERHOOD PROTECTORS BOOK #12

New York Times & USA Today
Bestselling Author

ELLE JAMES

MONTANA SEAL'S
MAIL-ORDER
BRIDE

BROTHERHOOD PROTECTORS

NEW YORK TIMES BESTSELLING AUTHOR
ELLE JAMES

CHAPTER 1

GAVIN STARED out the window of the foreman's office as Hank and Sadie Patterson climbed out of their dark, full-sized SUV. Sadie opened the back door and fiddled inside, finally lifting baby Emma out of her car seat and into her arms.

His chest tightened, and his breathing lodged in his throat. It happened every time he saw Hank, Sadie and Emma together. When he'd been on active duty, he'd thought himself immune to needing a family. Now, approaching thirty-five, single and missing part of one leg, Gavin guessed his chances at what Hank had were slim to none.

"Blackstock!" a female voice sounded behind him.

Gavin started and spun to face Lori Mize, one of the residents at the Brighter Days Rehabilitation Ranch. She leaned heavily on her good leg, her arms crossed over her chest, her bright blue eyes narrowed.

"What's wrong with you? I called your name four times before you turned around. Did one of your *other* disabilities have anything to do with your hearing?"

Anyone without disabilities wouldn't have gotten away with her comment, but Lori knew he was there for the same reasons she'd come to Montana. Transitioning to civilian life after a catastrophic injury such as they'd both received had proven more difficult than they'd imagined. This ranch had better results than most facilities that tried to prepare them for life outside of Uncle Sam's military.

But then Gavin could have never dreamed he'd lose a limb, ending his career as a US Navy SEAL. He turned back to the happy picture Hank, Sadie and Emma made.

Lori crossed to the window and stood beside him. "So stinkin' happy. Almost makes my sweet tooth hurt." She sighed. "But I can't begrudge them their happiness. They deserve it after all they've been through."

"Agreed." Gavin continued to stare at the family. "Ever wonder where you'd be in your life if you hadn't lost your leg?"

Lori's lips pressed into a thin line. "I'd hoped to be married with a kid or two by now." She glanced toward him. "You?"

He shrugged. "What's it matter, anyway? We are who we are."

Her brow furrowing, Lori faced him and cocked her head to one side. "And what is that supposed to mean?"

He nodded toward the Pattersons. "We'll probably never have what they have."

"I don't know what you're talking about. I lost my leg, not my reproductive parts." She patted her belly. "I haven't given up hope on having kids." Her gaze slipped from his and went to Hank.

He shot her a sideways glance. "Interesting. You didn't say anything about marriage."

She lifted one shoulder. "I figure if a man can't accept me for how I am now, I don't need one. I can have a baby without a man," she muttered beneath her breath, but loud enough Gavin caught the words. "Though it would be a lot easier with one."

"Right. I was hellbent on being a lifer as a SEAL. I didn't want to get married and drag a wife around from duty station to duty station while I deployed eleven months out of the year. I didn't think it would be fair."

She glanced at him, one eyebrow arched. "And now that you're not deploying, why don't you date and find you a woman to settle down with?"

"You want to go out with me?" Gavin asked, knowing the answer before she gave it.

"Oh, hell no." Lori shook her head. "It would be like going out with my older brother. Eww." She studied him. "But there's no reason you can't find someone."

He snorted. "In case you haven't noticed, there aren't that many women around Eagle Rock, Montana. And most of them know I'm missing a leg."

"So?" Lori's brow dipped low on her forehead. "You're saying you don't think a woman can love you because you're one leg short of a pair? Hell, what's that mean for my chances? I'm short one leg, too" She flung her arm in the air. "Guess I'm destined to hit a sperm bank, if I want kids."

"Be serious."

She looked at the Pattersons again and gave a deep sigh. "You want kids?"

He nodded, his gaze going to baby Emma.

The ranch's physical therapist Hannah Kendricks stepped out of the house, smiling at Hank and Sadie. She took Emma in her arms and tickled the baby beneath her chin.

"Sure, I want kids," Gavin said. "But more than that, I want a partner in life. Someone to come home to, to share the ups and downs."

"Someone to love?"

"If I could have it all, yes." Gavin turned away from the scene and paced the office floor. "Maybe I should move to a city where I could meet more women. Women who would be tolerant of my...shortcomings."

Lori gave a bark of laughter. "You? In a city?" She

shook her head. "Not happening. You'd shrivel up and die." Her gaze never left him. "You're serious, aren't you?" She touched his arm. "Gavin, you're a good guy. Your gal just hasn't made her appearance yet."

"And she's not going to. Not out here."

"Shoot, Gavin, how many women have you dated since coming to Montana?"

"None," he said, his tone flat. "There aren't that many out here."

"Maybe you should broaden your horizons. Have you signed up with an online dating site?" Lori asked.

"Hell, no. Have you?" Gavin shot back at her.

"I don't want a mate so badly I'm ready to put myself out there." She shook a finger at him. "Besides, we weren't talking about me. We were talking about your situation. Gavin Blackstock, you're lonely."

"I'm not getting any younger," he said, his jaw hardening. He didn't like admitting that he was lonely. But Lori had hit the nail on the head. "I don't want to put my name on some site, and then meet a woman who has expectations of meeting a whole man. I want to be up front with a woman. She needs to know the truth before we even meet."

"Then do it," Lori urged. "There has to be someone out there for you."

"But I don't want to date. Why can't a guy advertise for a wife, get one and be done with the whole damn thing? Courting is a pain in the ass." He ran a hand through his hair. "Oh, forget about it. It doesn't matter, anyway."

"Gavin, sounds like what you need is a mail-order bride." Lori grinned and plopped down at Gavin's desk and booted up the computer. "I bet there's a place on the internet where you can advertise for a bride. We just have to look."

"No. I'm fine being alone. Sorry I ever opened my mouth."

"The hell you are. Look at you, mooning over Hank and Sadie." Lori clicked on the keys and brought up a browser window. She typed in mail-order bride and waited as suggestions popped up on the screen. "Wow. Who knew there were that many porn sites for mail-order brides? Dang..."

"Just shut it down. I'm not interested. Besides, she'd have to be pretty desperate to agree to be a mail-order bride."

"Wait, here's a site that looks legit." Lori paused and read through the information provided. "All the applicants are vetted to make sure they aren't felons or already married. If they're foreign, they have to have a valid passport. They suggest the parties meet online first, and then arrange a meet and greet in person. If the parties are in agreement, a special license can be obtained, or they can fly to Vegas for a quick wedding." Lori clicked more keys.

"What are you doing?"

"I'm entering your information." She glanced at

him, running her gaze over him from top to toe. "You're what…six-feet tall?"

"Six-one," he corrected. "But stop right now. I'm not interested in marrying a stranger. We might not even be compatible."

"You can enter exactly what you want in a bride. A full list of requirements." She cocked an eyebrow. "So, what's top on your list?"

"Damn it, Lori. I'm not ordering a bride."

She acted as though he hadn't spoken, her lips pursing as she typed. "Must be female with a Y chromosome." She laughed. "You never know."

"Lori…" Gavin gave her his most dangerous tone.

She still wasn't listening. "Must love horses. Must want children. Willing to work hard." She smiled up at Gavin. "Am I right?"

"Yes, but you're missing the point." He clenched his fists. "I'm not marrying a stranger."

Lori glared at him. "You're the one missing the point. If you don't put yourself out there, you won't get anything." She raised her cell phone and snapped a picture of him. Then she typed more information onto the screen and hit enter.

Gavin stared over her shoulder. "What did you just do?" A screen popped up congratulating Gavin Blackstock on joining the site. "You didn't."

Lori pushed away from the desk and out of range of Gavin's hands. "Now, you wait and see if you get a live one. I'll be back later to go through the responses with you."

He scowled. "I'll reject every one of them. You're wasting my time and theirs."

"At least, give it a week and see what comes of it."

"I'm not giving it anything. I'm not ordering my bride through the internet like a goddamn bag of dogfood."

Lori patted his cheek. "Just you wait. I have a feeling about this. I think you're going to get lucky and find the right woman for you." She smiled. "Then you can thank me." She winked and darted up from the chair before Gavin could grab her and strangle the life out of her.

What the hell had Lori gotten him into? He leaned over the computer and read the ad.

Wanted: Bride to live on a ranch in Montana. Must be willing to work hard and bear children. Undaunted groom, one leg short of a pair, loyal and respectful.

"Great. I sound like a pathetic, desperate loser."

Lori laughed. "I was thinking you sounded more like a Labrador retriever." She patted him on the arm. "I bet you get a number of hits before the end of the week."

"Whoever answers that ad has to be another pathetic and desperate loser." Gavin shook his head. "I'm not going through with this."

"Give it a chance," Lori said. "At least, see who

responds. Who knows? You might find the woman of your dreams."

Gavin snorted. "More like my nightmares."

OLIVIA AURELIA ST. George sat in the church after everyone else had gone except her best friend Lilianna and her bodyguard Collin. She stared down at her hands with the white handkerchief crumpled in her grip and studied the contrast between it and her black dress. Guilt stabbed her in the heart. They had been good men. She hadn't loved them, but that hadn't been a requirement. They had been willing to marry her. "This is all my fault."

Lilianna covered her hands with one of her own. "You can't say that. You didn't drive the car that killed Andrew. Someone else did."

"If he hadn't agreed to marry me, he wouldn't have been where he was when that car hit him."

"Again, it's not your fault. They'll catch the driver," Lilianna said. "Just wait." Her words were hopeful, but the tone wasn't.

Olivia shook her head. "When? They never found the man who pushed Ian into the path of an oncoming bus." She looked up into Lilianna's eyes. "Two fiancés, two deaths. This is not a coincidence. The law states that if I don't find a husband and start producing heirs by my 30th birthday, the throne goes to the next in line. It's hopeless."

"You'll find a husband. And you still have time to get pregnant," Lilianna took her hands in hers. "Don't give up now. You have ten months to make it all happen."

Ten months. To get married and have a child. Ten months. It would take a miracle to find a man who would agree to marry her when both fiancés she'd had were now dead. What man in his right mind would sign up for that?

"Why don't you look at one of those online dating sites?" Lilianna suggested. She pulled out her cell phone and searched online dating.

"I don't really have much time to date. One month to marry and get started making a baby isn't going to work. I might as well give up."

"No way." Lilianna stared across at her. "You can't let your cousin Rupert take the throne. He's not fit to be a ruler."

"And I am? I can't even find a man to marry and propagate the line." Olivia sighed. "I hate the thought that this would disappoint my father. I know how much he would have wanted me to be the next queen of Lastovia, given the circumstances of my brother's demise."

"Darling, he groomed you since you were born."

Olivia closed her eyes for a moment. "He groomed my brother. Besides, we're only figureheads anymore these days. I wish it still wasn't so important who rules."

"Because people looked up to your father, your brother and now, you. In such trying times, they like to have a monarch who understands their needs and represents them in the world."

"Sometimes, I wish I was just a regular person. Then I'd fall in love and live happily ever after."

Lilianna snorted. "There's no guarantee on the happily-ever-after, even for us mere mortals." Lilianna frowned and keyed into her phone. "Okay... so you don't have time to do the dating roulette game. How about one of those mail-order bride sites? You can skip the dating and get right down to the marriage and children part."

"The only men who sign up for those sites are desperate."

"Exactly," Lilianna said. "No questions asked, just get married and make a baby."

Olivia shook her head. "I can't do this."

"Just humor me, will you?" Lilianna said. "Here you go. Bachelor number one lives in England. He's a professor of history and likes playing cribbage. Sounds boring, but manageable." She scrolled down through the man's details.

Olivia grabbed the phone from her and looked at the man's picture. "No way. He has to be sixty years old. And look, he doesn't want children."

Lilianna took the phone back from Olivia.

"Scratch bachelor number one. Oh, look. Bachelor number two is from Louisiana in the US. He's twice divorced, has two teenaged sons and is looking for a woman who likes hunting and race car driving." She looked up. "He has two sons. That means he's fertile. He's not horrible to look at, and he's a mechanic, so he's bound to be good at fixing things."

"I'm not into hunting, and speed makes me nervous." She shook her head. "Besides, he probably doesn't want to start over with an infant if he already has teenaged sons. Give it up, Lilianna."

"I refuse to have your cousin as my king." She kept looking at the phone. "Wait, I've got the man for you. He's never been married."

"No woman would have him...?"

"He's good-looking," Lilianna went on.

"Then he's probably a man who always has to be in control. Maybe even abusive."

"He's from the US, the state of Montana." Lilianna switched apps on her phone. "Where is Montana?"

"A state in the northwest. Known for its cold weather and miles and miles of nothing. There's not much out there, until you get to the western side of the state where all the mountains are. Even then, not many people live in Montana, from what I recall of my geography class."

"Wouldn't that be perfect?" Lilianna's face lit in a grin. "Sounds like it's way out in the middle of nowhere. A place you could get lost in. Whoever is sabotaging you won't find you there." She practically jumped up and down on her seat. "It's just what you need."

"I'm not going to Montana. I'm not marrying a stranger," Olivia said.

Lilianna switched back to the mail-order bride app and held up her hand. "Listen to this. If this isn't perfect, I don't know what is." She wiped the smile off her face and read out loud.

Wanted: Bride to live on a ranch in Montana. Must be willing to work hard and bear children.

"He sounds like a cowboy from way back in the old American west of the 1800s."

An image of a man wearing a cowboy hat and chaps rose in Olivia's mind. She wouldn't admit that she was intrigued. She'd spent many an evening watching old westerns on her television and had dreamed like many young girls of being rescued by a man on a white horse and riding off into the sunset.

"Look at him," Lilianna said. "He's even good looking. That strong chin and piercing eyes." She sighed. "If you don't go after him, I just might."

Olivia took the phone from her and glanced down at the image, hating to admit Lilianna was right. The man looked at her as if staring into her very soul. Awareness rippled through her body, coiling tightly in her belly.

"Caught your interest, didn't he," Lilianna whispered.

He had.

Olivia read the ad again.

Wanted: Bride to live on a ranch in Montana. Must be willing to work hard and bear children.

She scrolled further down to the part Lilianna hadn't read aloud.

Undaunted groom, one leg short of a pair, loyal and respectful.

She frowned, squinted and read it again. "You didn't read this part."

Lilianna leaned over her shoulder. "I didn't see it."

"What do you think this means—one leg short of a pair?"

"One leg short..." Lilianna's eyes rounded. "He only has one leg." Her face fell. "Well, shoot. And I thought we had a winner."

Olivia read more of the man's background. "Prior military, Purple Heart recipient. Lili, he lost his leg serving his country."

"Sounds like an honorable man. But we can keep looking." She reached for the cell phone.

Olivia turned away without giving it back. Something about the former warrior's face resonated with something deep inside herself. "No. I don't want to look at another."

"Fine. Then we go through a list of all of your acquaintances. Surely, there's a man amongst them who would make a suitable partner and father."

"No," Olivia said. "Actually, I think everything

you've been saying is right. I need to find a place where I can remain out of the public's eye."

"If you mean hide, then you're right." Lilianna paced the church aisle. "Where would be the best place to hide for the next ten months? Preferably a place with eligible bachelors. Eligible, desperate bachelors."

An idea took root and blossomed in Olivia's chest. She sat in one of the pews, hunkered over the phone and began typing.

"Olivia?"

"Shh." She kept typing, concentrating on what she wanted to say. Then she held up the phone, snapped a picture of herself and submitted her response.

"Olivia?" Lilianna snatched the phone from her hands. "What have you done?"

"I think I just accepted a proposal of marriage." Her heart pounded against her ribs, and she felt just a little queasy. But not nearly as nauseated as she'd felt every time she'd said yes to her two previous fiancés. What she'd just done was perhaps the most spontaneous and...crazy thing she'd ever done in her life. But sometimes, a person had to step outside the lines in order to make things happen.

"Sweetie, what have you done?"

"You can read my response. It's out there, but I didn't use my full name. I used the name Aurelia George."

Lilianna found her response and fell into a pew, her face pale.

"*Woman with biological clock ticking seeks groom with a family in mind. Willing to work hard and bear children. When can we meet?*"

"Oh, dear Lord. You're kidding, right?" Lilianna shook her head and the stared at Olivia. "Please tell me this is all a bad dream."

Olivia's lips twisted. "Lili, this was your idea. Don't tell me you're having second thoughts."

"But he's only got one leg," she whispered.

"Therefore, he's got to be a little desperate. I need a man who's just desperate enough make this work." Olivia smiled, feeling more lighthearted than she had in months. She waved to the man standing guard at the door to the little church. "Collin," she called out.

The man checked out the window beside the exit before he turned to join Olivia in the aisles. "Yes, ma'am."

"Are you up for a visit to the US?" She slid a side-eye in his direction. Olivia had done a thorough background check on Collin O'Bannon, but she couldn't remember everything. Only that he'd come highly recommended as a bodyguard. "You're from somewhere in the US, correct?"

"Yes. Maine."

"Good." She leaned close. "Ever been to Montana?"

He nodded. "Went elk hunting there with my father."

Hunting was a good, outdoor sport. But she needed him to be closer than a neighbor, if she was going to pull this off. "Ever done any ranching?"

"As a matter of fact…no."

"Do you know anything about horses or cattle?"

"Only that one we eat, and the other we don't."

She chewed on her bottom lip.

"You're not seriously considering marrying this one-legged cowboy from Montana, are you?"

A hope bloomed in Olivia's chest and spread outward until it lit her face with a smile. "That's exactly what I'm considering." She grabbed Lilianna's hand. "Come on, we have a lot to do in a short amount of time, if Mr. Gavin Blackstock accepts my response."

ABOUT THE AUTHOR

ELLE JAMES also writing as MYLA JACKSON is a *New York Times* and *USA Today* Bestselling author of books including cowboys, intrigues and paranormal adventures that keep her readers on the edges of their seats. When she's not at her computer, she's traveling, snow skiing, boating, or riding her ATV, dreaming up new stories. Learn more about Elle James at www.ellejames.com

Website | Facebook | Twitter | GoodReads |
Newsletter | BookBub | Amazon

Or visit her alter ego Myla Jackson at
mylajackson.com
Website | Facebook | Twitter | Newsletter

Follow Me!
www.ellejames.com
ellejamesauthor@gmail.com

ALSO BY ELLE JAMES

Shadow Assassin

Brotherhood Protectors Colorado

SEAL Salvation (#1)

Rocky Mountain Rescue (#2)

Ranger Redemption (#3)

Tactical Takeover (#4)

Colorado Conspiracy (#5)

Rocky Mountain Madness (#6)

Free Fall (#7)

Colorado Cold Case (#8)

Fool's Folly (#9)

Colorado Free Rein (#10)

Brotherhood Protectors

Montana SEAL (#1)

Bride Protector SEAL (#2)

Montana D-Force (#3)

Cowboy D-Force (#4)

Montana Ranger (#5)

Montana Dog Soldier (#6)

Montana SEAL Daddy (#7)

Montana Ranger's Wedding Vow (#8)

Montana SEAL Undercover Daddy (#9)

Cape Cod SEAL Rescue (#10)

Montana SEAL Friendly Fire (#11)

Montana SEAL's Mail-Order Bride (#12)

Driving Force (#4)

Tactical Force (#5)

Disruptive Force (#6)

Mission: Six

One Intrepid SEAL

Two Dauntless Hearts

Three Courageous Words

Four Relentless Days

Five Ways to Surrender

Six Minutes to Midnight

Hearts & Heroes Series

Wyatt's War (#1)

Mack's Witness (#2)

Ronin's Return (#3)

Sam's Surrender (#4)

Take No Prisoners Series

SEAL's Honor (#1)

SEAL'S Desire (#2)

SEAL's Embrace (#3)

SEAL's Obsession (#4)

SEAL's Proposal (#5)

SEAL's Seduction (#6)

Hot Zone (#3)

Hot Velocity (#4)

Cajun Magic Mystery Series

Voodoo on the Bayou (#1)

Voodoo for Two (#2)

Deja Voodoo (#3)

Cajun Magic Mysteries Books 1-3

SEAL Of My Own

Navy SEAL Survival

Navy SEAL Captive

Navy SEAL To Die For

Navy SEAL Six Pack

Devil's Shroud Series

Deadly Reckoning (#1)

Deadly Engagement (#2)

Deadly Liaisons (#3)

Deadly Allure (#4)

Deadly Obsession (#5)

Deadly Fall (#6)

Covert Cowboys Inc Series

Triggered (#1)

Taking Aim (#2)

Bodyguard Under Fire (#3)

Cowboy Resurrected (#4)

Navy SEAL Justice (#5)

Navy SEAL Newlywed (#6)

High Country Hideout (#7)

Clandestine Christmas (#8)

Thunder Horse Series

Hostage to Thunder Horse (#1)

Thunder Horse Heritage (#2)

Thunder Horse Redemption (#3)

Christmas at Thunder Horse Ranch (#4)

Demon Series

Hot Demon Nights (#1)

Demon's Embrace (#2)

Tempting the Demon (#3)

Lords of the Underworld

Witch's Initiation (#1)

Witch's Seduction (#2)

The Witch's Desire (#3)

Possessing the Witch (#4)

Stealth Operations Specialists (SOS)

Nick of Time

Alaskan Fantasy

Boys Behaving Badly Anthologies

Rogues (#1)

Blue Collar (#2)

Pirates (#3)

Stranded (#4)

First Responder (#5)

Blown Away

Warrior's Conquest

Enslaved by the Viking Short Story

Conquests

Smokin' Hot Firemen

Protecting the Colton Bride

Protecting the Colton Bride & Colton's Cowboy Code

Heir to Murder

Secret Service Rescue

High Octane Heroes

Haunted

Engaged with the Boss

Cowboy Brigade

Time Raiders: The Whisper

Bundle of Trouble

Killer Body

Operation XOXO

An Unexpected Clue

Baby Bling

Under Suspicion, With Child

Texas-Size Secrets

Cowboy Sanctuary

Lakota Baby

Dakota Meltdown

Beneath the Texas Moon

Made in the USA
Middletown, DE
27 February 2023

25816954R00146